PALINODE
"Keeper of Legends"
Zev Bronski

2024, TWB Press
https://www.twbpress.com

Table of Contents

Palinode:

From ancient Greek *palin* to Latin *palinōidia* then late 16th century English: A poem in which the poet retracts a view or sentiment expressed in a former poem. Translated to the 21st century version: a narrative in which the author contradicts a previous scientific theory or commonly accepted historical convictions.

Characters:

John Laden, The Conservator
Silas Vern, The Seeker
Yarpay, The Ancient One
Urmachiscan, One Who Falls Down
Kuma, The Healer
Toltec, The Architect
Airto, The Guide
Pilot, Anonymous
Banik, The Penitent
Chikaj, Creator of Flight
Chaben, The Confidant

Foreword

The inspiration for this book resulted from several unrelated but coincidental discoveries that occurred within the last few years. Recent developments in radiometric dating techniques used in geochronology suggest that accepted archaeological time scales for the presence of humans on earth are far more ancient than was previously considered possible. The expanded potential of human chronology allows for the emergence and evolution of civilizations that predated the earliest recorded Mesopotamian, Oriental, and Central American civilizations. On the coattails of the new radiometric dating techniques was an experiment at MIT that demonstrated amino acids could be used for data storage of things like images or even video. Thus, the essential premise of this palinode is that very ancient peoples have used anomalous non-coding genetic material to store libraries of information in the human genome that has persisted for a half million years. And what will that 'information' reveal?

There were giants in the earth in those days; and also after that, when the sons of God came unto the daughters of men, and they bare children to them, the same became mighty men which were of old, men of renown.

– Genesis 6:4

CHAPTER 1 - ACCELERATION

L ike his father, and his father's father before him, the hunter stepped deftly in the traces of his prey, comparing the shape and size of his oddly lobed foot with the jagged tracks of the small antelope. The imprints turned suddenly in the direction of a steep ridge where the creature's hooves pressed deep in the red earth and the casual tempo of alternating right and left hooves became a staccato of side-by-side leaping, as the animal teeter-tottered its way along the incline as though suspended by an invisible pendulum.

The hunter hurried his pace, making the ascent with a burst of energy that propelled him in a zigzag pattern, back and forth, from rocky outcrop to thickly rooted handholds until he emerged at the mountain crest. He stood for a moment catching his breath after the exertion and surveyed the broad horizon. The dense morning light etched its way across the landscape, peeling back the night, revealing a land that was raw and exposed. The forest creatures cried in unison as the downy blanket was cast aside unveiling a new day.

Picking up the trail once again, the hunter moved quickly, following the drainages from the low mountains where cool mineral water bubbled from artesian wells down to the lush valleys at the stream's convergence, as boiling water polished the river rock into exquisite gems.

How many cycles of sun and moon, monsoon and drought, ween and rut, migration and return had repeated since the days of the ancient ones? "The world is kind," Yarpay thought. "Why do things leave? I never want to leave."

Moving in a steady rhythm, he entered a phalanx of Brazil nut and banana trees where the antelope had concealed itself beneath a curtain of large waxy leaves, glistening with morning dew and yellow pearls of insect engulfing amber. Panting heavily, the antelope stood motionless under the shade of the banana tree. Having lost its fanged incisors over the course of a half million years of isolated tranquility, the hapless creature could not venture the kind of ferocious counterattack that made its ancestors the terror of the forest floor, but instead was resigned to trembling in the shadows, awaiting its demise.

In a single fluid movement, honed to perfection from his earliest days, a virtual Sandy Kofax of the Holocene, Yarpay raised his axe and unleashed its fearful purpose. The axe tore through the thick morning air, barely grazing the beast's haunches as the famished weapon vanished into the forest beyond. The startled antelope leaped into the air, caught himself, and then launched into the protection of the forest shroud.

Yarpay's stomach convulsed as he watched his

meal make its escape. Though tree fruits and nuts were in abundance, it was the healing power of the animal's flesh that he craved. As he searched for his axe amongst the dense foliage, he considered the failed attack.

Yarpay was gifted with a powerful memory. Unlike other members of his tribe, he could replay the details of his hunting exploits in sound and in color. Over and over again he would consider the position of his feet, the trajectory and velocity of his axe, the extension of his arm, and the devastating impact of the axe hitting its intended target.

This unusual mental ability not only conserved precious calories that might otherwise be spent refining his throwing technique but saved him from shoulder injuries resulting from repeated practice with his axe. His capacity to extrapolate himself from the physical environment and recreate himself in an entirely imagined world was highly adaptive and altogether unique to his species.

What had gone wrong? Yarpay's hunger was a harsh and unforgiving critic. He re-imagined the morning's hunt in the batting cage of his mind, studying every nuance of his environment from the gentle breeze that carried the sweet aroma of plumeria to his gratified nostrils, to the rivulets of red ants that ran uncontested through the decaying leaves of the living earth.

Pondering his latest misadventure, he studied the columns of light that descended through the forest canopy, drawing negative images of leaves and branches on the ground. "The sun is teaching me a lesson," he thought.

He cast his gaze skyward, momentarily peering directly at the orb of the sun as it passed behind a towering fir tree. He closed his eyes in pain and covered his face with his hands. Through the darkness, the blazing image of the fir tree glowed brightly beneath his eyelids.

"Everything has its opposite. Where there is light, there is also shadow. And in this momentary failure, there is also understanding and growth."

And then a curious thing happened. The self that he imagined in his waking dreams, like a small miniature idol that he could manipulate, moving the piece across the war board of his intellect to encounter enemies and wild game, became suddenly realized.

In the same fashion that he had visualized a shadow self to hunt and do battle in the dream space of his consciousness, he imagined that he might also be a shadow of something still greater. "Am I a dream?" he muttered.

At the borderlands of pre-memory and inspiration, Yarpay found self-awareness.

CHAPTER 2 – JUNK YARD

John Laden removed his glasses and reached into his desk drawer for an 8-ounce bottle of optical cleaner that he kept at the ready. "Hmm...empty," he said to himself. "Maybe this will work," he thought, as he grabbed a container of disinfectant he used for his keyboard. He sprayed the lenses and wiped them clean with a polishing cloth, but they smeared with an oily residue that quickly condensed to a dull pink haze. "Not so good." He placed the fouled glasses back on his nose and stared at his computer with dissatisfaction. "I think it's time for a break." He removed the glasses, and setting them aside, he took a crumpled brown paper bag from his briefcase and set it on his desk.

From down the hall he could hear a cacophony of voices tumbling along the linoleum floor like a wrath of bowling pins. Some of the new hires were gathering with the department head in the Anthropoid Engineering unit to embark on a luncheon outing. As they exchanged introductions and shared their stories of academic and professional conquests, the conglomeration of new talent spread across the lobby into discrete cells of hopeful collaborators, friendly rivals, and the inevitable prima donnas who competed for positions in any such research institution.

Who would rise to the top? Who would harness their education and natural gifts and create something new? During a similar gathering years before, one of John's mentors once conferred an unscientific observation that, over time, he had come to trust as a fact that was as real as the inverse square law.

He had said, "You know, John, when you get old like me, you begin to see the world in the rearview mirror. When I was speeding along the highway, I was concerned with the obstacles in my immediate path. I didn't pull over for rest stops or take advantage of scenic lookouts on my journey. My focus was always the horizon, and if truth be told, much of the time I was moving faster than what the traffic conditions would normally permit.

"I have seen a great many people move through this institution and made some good friends over the years, but there is something that I recognized about human nature that I now understand as a hard rule. Only eight percent of the human population creates everything that you see around you...from the car you drive, to the phone you use, or the bodega on the corner where you get your liverwurst sandwich. Just eight percent. Then there are the twelve percent of the population who are the helpers to the eight percent. These are the people who implement the plans, manage the schedules, do the inventory...the whole of society is being propelled by just twenty percent of the population. You might ask, what of the remaining eighty percent? They go through the world as if in a dream. Life happens to them, and they don't know why. These new recruits...you'll see that they break into the 8 percent, 12 percent, 80 percent distribution. You just watch."

As John sat in his office, he listened intently to the growing throng. The excited conversations rose and fell until one by one, the voices dropped off, and the orchestra of murmuring was corralled into submission by a single commanding voice holding court over the entire assemblage. The voice was unfamiliar, which piqued John's curiosity, prompting him to rise from his seat and lean outside the door of his office, bracing himself against the inner doorframe with both hands, the way a train conductor might suspend himself between two passenger cars as it decelerates into the station.

To his surprise, he witnessed a rather unimposing young man with wavy brown hair, white collared shirt and argyle cashmere vest, and steam-pressed blue oxfords. The man had a modest, unaffected manner about him and a warm engaging smile. Yet, the clarion resonance of his voice was captivating, almost hypnotic.

"Interesting," John murmured. "I guess they have found their alpha." He returned to his desk where his sack lunch had been patiently waiting and recalled the halcyon days of his youth, when his laboratory was a hive of excitement, and geneticists vied for a place on his team as the surest pathway to future success. And indeed, his lab had been an incubator for the careers of many researchers who carved their initials over the threshold and moved on to achieve celebrity. John sometimes thought of himself as the station-keeper for one of the Butterfield stagecoach outposts. His employees would race into the station in a whirlwind. After being replenished with a pint of corn whiskey, a bowl full of chili, and a team of fresh horses, away they went in a cloud of ambition.

"Those were good times," he quietly reminisced.

John was a paleo-geneticist and one of the early advocates of a technology called vestigial phenotype rescue that was now rapidly becoming obsolete. He and his colleagues scoured the human genome, searching for "silenced genes" that might be reactivated into protein coding sequences to serve contemporary purposes. Some critics of the practice called it Dumpster Diving, but for a while, the salvage operation had an energetic and devoted following of hobbyists and professionals who viewed their work as an act of historic preservation by harvesting the latent evolutionary energy stored in the genome. A coffee cup on his desk was branded with the ironic label: "What Would Dino Do?"

The notion that all of life's problems had been previously solved and wrapped up neatly with a ribbon of DNA was perhaps over optimistic, but scientific revolutions are rarely inspired by the reasonable. John believed that silenced genes were nature's great pyramids. The travail of generations of skilled artisans and chattel slaves grinding away at ten-ton limestone blocks produced monuments that were mysterious in their purpose and awe-inspiring in their scale and grandeur. The luster had given way to time, but the intention shined through.

Phenotypes like the vestigial gills or a once-proud tail that communicated a sense of curiosity and fun, had vanished into a morass of editors notes and deletions, subsumed by a legion of false starts and dead ends that were a response to the onslaught of a rapidly changing planet. The code was still there, but their joyful and occasionally sinister expression in the artifice of bone and flesh had disappeared.

One of his team's success stories was in salvaging the plica semilunaris. In most humans, the structure is a fold in the conjunctiva of the inner corner of the eye, akin to a nictating membrane, or third eyelid. The membrane was likely used by humans to see underwater when they were an aquatic species of apes. John and his team were successful in resurrecting the trait for the benefit of commercial astronauts so that asteroid miners could preserve their vision on long missions to and from the asteroid belt. Previous long-haul astronauts had suffered from deformation of the eyeball after long periods in weightlessness. The addition of the membrane offered a kind of optical splint that preserved the integrity of the astronaut's vision.

Much of his team's early work was underwritten by the aerospace industry. The development of the Mach-Woodward impulse engine had opened the solar system to human exploration, making mankind a space-faring species, at last. Would-be adventurers poured into space academies by the thousands, seeking their fortune in the stars, not unlike the Conquistadors who crowded onto the decks of Spanish galleons in search of treasure in the New World. Indeed, the predicted wealth available in the asteroid belt was more than all the precious metals on earth, and the launch of every new spaceship sent the financial markets catapulting. Even the European Southern Observatory's Very Large Telescope (ESO VLT) was commandeered for the purpose of detecting heavy metal gases in the atmospheres of near-earth asteroids, the low hanging fruit of the celestial mining business. Who would find the next Potosi, or the next Guanajuato? The trades were rife with speculation.

As in previous periods of mining frenzy, the greatest fortunes were made by the space outfitters. The suppliers of laser drills, freeze dried food stuffs, space suits, detonators and blasting caps, and especially the financiers, made huge sums of money.

One of John's proudest achievements in this regard earned him a Dawkins prize, and an all-expense paid trip to Jamaica. In what was considered one of the outstanding inter-species appropriations of the time, he skillfully procured sequences from a Kodiak bear named Tolstoy, who was a much beloved resident of the San Diego Zoo, which allowed deep space astronauts to hibernate as well as recycle their own urine. Fortuitously, the same sequence also led to a cure for gout. John typically shunned the limelight, but the effusion of respectful admirers, not to mention the blank check he received from his investors, was at once euphoric if not long-lived.

His triumph in appropriating the bear's hibernation scheme made him attempt the same thing with the genes from a Wood frog, which had the uncanny ability to be frozen entirely and re-animate during the spring thaw. The experiments ended in failure when the human test subjects became afflicted with Type 1 diabetes and long-term sugar psychosis, as they lost their ability to store glycogens in the liver. The failure caused John to abandon his research in cross-species genetics and focus on his first love of silenced genes.

But that was a long time ago, and the state of the art had moved on, as it always did. His little stagecoach outpost was eventually bypassed by the steam engines of modern genomics. To many, vestigial phenotype rescue was the equivalent of an abandoned mine that had given up the last of its precious ore. Sifting through the tailings was unglamorous and unprofitable. Stalwarts like John, however, persisted. He felt that his colleagues dismissed his efforts like a dusty old prospector who stubbornly refused to come down off the mountain and had become more of an eccentric hermit and teller of tall tales than a productive miner. He made no effort to convince people otherwise.

Nevertheless, the corporation let him keep his desk and his job because of his contributions to the company, but no one was beating down his door. Occasionally, someone from the human resources department would stop by to see if they could "borrow" a chair or use one of John's storage cabinets. The retreating tide of staplers, computer monitors, and pen sets continued to drift away, but the current never seemed to flow in reverse, instead, leaving his office looking like a small fleet of fishing trawlers leaning to one side, abandoned to the indignity of the mud flats. He had become a curiosity of sorts. Yet, he refused to gracefully acquiesce to the inheritance of Paul Bunyan and John Henry. He had staked his claim, and he would defend it.

CHAPTER 3 – PRANDIUM INTERRUPTUS

John had initially begun searching for vestigial phenotypes using a music recognition algorithm called *Tin Ear* he once used as a kid in grade school. Instead of comparing time and frequency domains to a catalog of songs from the hit parade, he adapted the program to compare genetic sequences to known human traits, such as skin and hair, otherwise known as equivalent homologies. The only drawback to the technique was that unfamiliar datasets slipped through the cracks based on the completeness of the genetic archive. Although his inability to identify a song belonging to the Mystic Knights of the Oingo Boingo was only frustrating, the absence of an equivalent recognized trait from a seemingly promising polygenic sequence could be downright confounding.

During a typical analytical run, some of these unfamiliar sequences were purged into a virtual holding bin for later evaluation, much like a burned mozzarella stick getting jettisoned off the conveyor belt at the Tasty Cheese factory.

As he sat at his desk munching on a liverwurst sandwich, he leisurely scrolled through the sidelined sequences, looking for any evidence of code that was relevant to human features.

"Oh...what's this?" he said to the computer screen.

A dense packet of seemingly non-coding DNA presented itself as a sequence of potential interest. "Why haven't I noticed you before?" He took another bite of his sandwich. "You're not meat, you're not bone...something else..."

As he studied the code, he recognized that it resembled a particular kind of sequence he had once isolated from an endangered Hawaiian pheasant. On that occasion he discovered the genetic sequence coded for a very sophisticated mating ritual that included singing and clicking noises, rhythmic dancing, scratching of the earth, displays of color, and pheromone signaling.

"Could it be a courtship ritual?" he mused. "A war dance, perhaps?" Certain kinds of human ceremonial activity had been so often repeated in association with specific life affirming or life-threatening events that the repetitive behavior was instantiated in the genome.

"Perhaps it's not as esoteric as a coronation or a marriage, maybe it's something more elemental." He allowed his imagination to drift on the tide of possibilities. Then he almost blushed at his own ego. "Could this be..?" He was embarrassed to take ownership of his idea. The missing link of behavioral genetics was the code that underpinned the behavior for the creation of fire—the behavioral adaptation that paved the way for modern man.

The very thought made him giddy with excitement. Fire had allowed his ancestors to take back the night from the thieving jackals and ravenous predators that tormented them. It enabled the roasting of plants and flesh, which made their digestion more efficient, freeing them from endless rumination. It gave them the ability to clear large areas of land through controlled burning, ridding themselves of insects and pestilence while also preparing the soil for agriculture. *Fire.* The mother of all inventions.

"Excuse me, Dr. Laden?"

"Oh...yes, I apologize. I didn't see you standing there." It took him more than a moment to disengage from his daydream and redirect his attention to his visitor. "Come in and sit down. I was just finishing my lunch." He made an effort to clear some old papers off of a swivel chair and gestured for the man to be seated. Then he realized that this was the very same argyle-vested gentleman who had previously captured his attention.

"My name is Silas Vern." He offered a handshake.

"Mr. Vern, to what do I owe this pleasure?"

Vern smiled. "I suppose in this case it's a what and also a why. I will start with the "what," which is your numerous citations in *Science* and *Nature*, which guided me like a trail of breadcrumbs that led me through my graduate work. And since there is no sense in beating around the bush, I may as well just tell you that the "why" as you have already surmised is that I would like to collaborate with you on a project that I began as a postdoc until I ran out of funding from the NIH last year. I believe you may be the only person who can understand what I've been up to. And if you'll bear with me, I would like to explain."

John had been on the receiving end of numerous research proposals over the years, some of them good, some bad, and some completely insane. Although he no longer controlled the purse-strings, he still had the ear of the funding committee, and at least some influence to move cheese from one maze to another.

"Alright, as Goldie Hawn used to say, sock it to me." He grinned at his little joke.

Vern just stared at him confused, not knowing the reference, then continued. "I've been using statistical analysis to investigate certain novel gene sequences that don't appear to conform to the evolutionary continuum of the genome. There are sequences that seem to suddenly appear without reference to history, and specifically, every one of these sequences corresponds to a kind of behavioral trope. For example, there is a sequence that appeared very late in the game, without historic precedents that seems to code for mathematical or abstract logic. Now, I understand that some folks would describe this as an example of punctuated equilibrium, but I think the evidence points to a certain amount of tinkering."

"Tinkering, you say?" John frowned.

"What I'm trying to say is that these sequences are artifacts, or what I call genoglyphs. They are the evidence of ancient peoples deliberately influencing the genome."

"I see. No wonder you lost your grant."

"Don't get me wrong, Dr. Laden. I'm not suggesting that ancient peoples had electroporators and thermal cyclers. That's not the point. What I am suggesting is that pre-industrial or very ancient civilizations may have inadvertently used viruses, or bacteria, or perhaps some species of plants to engineer the genome without understanding what genetic material is."

"Look, Mr. Vern, this is all very interesting—"

"Now hear me out." Silas's voice was insistent. "It would have appeared as magic to the ancients, but somehow, they stumbled onto a process that appears to have replicated modern genetic engineering techniques. The only thing they understood is that, by exposing individuals to certain plant tissues under specific conditions, they could elicit certain physical or behavioral traits.

"It's like the master sword makers who invented Damascus steel blades. They didn't know anything about the carbon nanotubes and cementite nanowires they were producing. All that the medieval blacksmiths knew is that through some accident, they stumbled onto this recipe, which produced unusual durability and superior cutting characteristics. It was a craft process of trial and error taking place over many centuries, and it changed the battlefield as well as the political landscape.

"They didn't understand the fundamentals of carbon chemistry or the molecular properties of vanadium, chromium, manganese, cobalt, and nickel. They were manipulating electron valencies and molecular bonding arrangements on a macroscopic scale without an appreciation of the underlying molecular machinery they were invoking. But they developed a keen intuition that resulted in weapons of unparalleled quality that modern masters have attempted and failed to replicate. No one questions whether the Syrian blade-smiths fashioned those blades because we have the provenience of their ownership."

Silas rested his case.

There was a part of John that enjoyed a good crackpot theory, and this was a doozy. Yet, he was unwilling to entirely dismiss what Silas was saying. If John had learned anything from life it was humility. After all, no less a scientist than Isaac Newton himself had dedicated over a third of his writings to the age-old pursuit of alchemy, with the goal of turning base metals into gold. Of course, two centuries later, Newton was vindicated, as it was discovered that lead can indeed be transmuted into gold, but only in a particle accelerator at extremely high energies, and consequently at very great expense, which entirely defeated the purpose of producing the gold in the first place.

Palinode – "Keeper of Legends"

"I like the fact that you're thinking about this in an unconventional way." John said it in a manner that he hoped did not sound condescending. "Frankly, I wish there were more people like you who were willing to risk their reputation for what they believe. But times have changed. People in this industry, as you have no doubt witnessed, are less tolerant of the outliers. They demand a procrustean intellectual conformity, while at the same instant, making quite ostentatious appeals for diversity. In these paradoxical times, an original thinker like you is a real problem.

"For some reason I can't explain, people have become very fragile. They are unwilling to have their beliefs challenged in any way. In the past, professional disagreements could get quite heated, but I never feared for my job. Today, that's not the case."

As he was gently consoling Silas, John was listening to his own words and thought, "What am I so afraid of? What do I have to lose that would be so unbearable if it were taken away from me? My job? My reputation? My income? What does any of it matter if I'm not moving forward and challenging my own assumptions?"

He studied the brilliant young Silas, who had taken the enormous gamble of exposing his ideas to a complete stranger, and had a sudden change of mind. "It's a fine line between genius and madness. Maybe this guy is on to something."

CHAPTER 4 – OVER THE HILLS AND FAR AWAY

An expression of trust deserved a similar exchange of confidence. Silas had left himself exposed by revealing his secret project. Sensing that their meeting was tilting awkwardly out of balance, John felt compelled to match Silas's level of candor and restore the state of equilibrium between the two with an offering.

"Can I show you something?" John said with constrained excitement.

Relieved by the invitation to continue their conversation instead of being ushered to the door, Silas eagerly responded, "Yes, of course. I apologize for my impertinence. I'm afraid that I've spent too much time talking about myself."

John leaned over his computer, which was quietly napping, and brought up the screen he had been working on prior to Silas's arrival. "There now. What do you think of that?"

Silas squeezed in next to John until they were standing nearly hip to hip and studied the lines of code arrayed across the monitor. "Silenced genes?"

John nodded approvingly. "Now look at the

sequences. Here...here, and again here. Do you see the data packets and the way they are arranged? I don't believe it's structural code, I think it's behavioral."

Silas stared at the monitor, straining with an expression that looked as though he had taken a slow drag off an unripe lime, and then he raised his eyebrows and slightly turned his head. "How could that be? What is this? I mean, what is the genetic context? How did you find it?"

John grinned. "Finally, somebody gets it."

"I was performing a global statistical analysis of some dead ends, and it was isolated as a potential pseudogene. I think it might be over a million years old."

"Yeah, but it's not behavioral either. I've seen this before."

John was somewhat taken aback at this revelation. "What do you mean...where have you seen it before?"

"Well, not this exactly, but I know what this is because I created something like this. I made an implant, you see."

John sat quietly stunned.

"When I was a postdoc, I shared an apartment with an old school friend of mine. Avery was his name. One evening we were enjoying some libations, as I was wont to do on occasion, and my friend turned to me and said he had made up his mind. He was definitely getting a tattoo.

"Keep in mind, this was before 3D luminescent

microcrystal tattoos you see today, which make kids look like one of those holographic marquees on the Indian casinos out along the highway. He was just talking about one of the old-timey, Polynesian style needle and ink jobs that make you look like a pirate.

"Anyway, we talked about it for a while, and he explains how Led Zeppelin changed his life, and Avery wants a permanent symbol of his devotion. By this time, I'm pretty drunk and I tell him not to bother with the tattoo, which is merely an affectation. And then I say, "If you really want something that's permanent, something that's more than just skin deep, I'll put Zeppelin into your DNA.

"I don't know if it was bravado or the alcohol talking. It was a joke, of course, but he immediately seized on the idea.

"'Can you actually do that?' he asked excitedly. Now I'm thinking, uh oh, what have I gotten myself into? But it's too late, the train has left the station, and it's barreling down the tracks. He's asking me all kinds of questions, and I'm beginning to seriously consider it, and I'm working out the mechanics in my head. As I'm figuring out the technical details, now I'm beginning to get excited. 'This could be really cool' I thought.

"Over the course of the next several weeks, I spent hundreds of hours converting pixels and audio code into base pairs of adenine, cystine, guanine, and thymine. I basically grabbed Zeppelin's 1976 concert movie, *The Song Remains the Same*, and inserted it directly into this guy's genome. It was non-coding DNA, of course, so that it wouldn't make any physical changes to his body, so it's basically encapsulated in a way that it can't cause any harm, but the information can be accessed by his neural mechanisms. Then I added some plant DNA to the five-prime end from a "locally sourced" marijuana plant to initiate the sequence. Whenever he smokes a bowl, the THC molecule from the plant essentially pushes the play button on the five-prime and starts the movie, painting the images and sound onto his occipital lobe."

"But...but...that's unethical," John managed to say.

"Yeah, I know," Silas responded dismissively. "But I'm guessing you haven't refused any of the residuals from that grizzly bear piss thing you did."

John was put on the defensive as their roles suddenly reversed. "That work was carried out under the supervision of the National Institute of Ethical Standards for Human Research under the strictest of standards, and—"

"Look, John..." Silas interjected, "we're both adults here. You and I both know that the arbitrary intervention of a bureaucratic office doesn't make a thing right or wrong. Those inter-species experiments were clearly banned, and have been since the 70s, but the mining cartel was on your side, so they rammed it through. Big surprise. Don't get me wrong, that was a great accomplishment, and it was important work, too. I admire it. I really do. That's part of the reason I'm here, but don't pretend that the grudging consent of some corrupt functionary is the equivalent of ethics, because it's not."

John was back on his heels. He wasn't accustomed to being challenged in his own lab.

"I haven't come here to argue with you about past mistakes." Silas changed his voice to a more conciliatory tone. "What I'm trying to tell you is that the sequence you identified is an artifact. It was manufactured and inserted in the genome by someone. It has the hallmarks of a visual and auditory message, similar to the one that I produced, and if you are willing, I would like to help you decode it."

CHAPTER 5 – FOUNTAINS OF THE DEEP

Nearing the end of his journey, the familiar landmarks of home filled Yarpay with joy. A bluish haze of sweet burning mahogany bestowed a dreamlike halo of tranquility that hovered protectively over the glowing campfires and thatched wikiups. The hypnotic repetition of a leather-bound drum made the hidden movement of time reveal itself for a while, just like the chameleon that steps from a yellow leaf onto a mottled stone, and so briefly betrays its leafy disguise before assuming its new costume. The drum is accompanied by a flute formed from a discarded antler, its shrill pitch echoed by a pack of wild dogs that announce their suspect invitation to the curious who would seek their siren song beneath the forest canopy.

As he draws closer, Yarpay can hear the laughter of children at play, and smell the aroma of tender cuts of meat drenched in fermented garlic and smoked underground in juvenile banana leaves. He hesitates briefly at the perimeter of the encampment to admire the pageant of his home and then bounds toward the central hearth, the focal point of the world.

Yarpay is immediately embraced by the villagers who are eager to welcome him back into the clan. An elder ignites a branch of the Scorpion bush and flagellates Yarpay's back and legs with the smoldering leaves, while a young woman and apprentice to the elder rubs a mélange of citrus oils into his hair. The returned are always decontaminated in this way, ridding them of the parasites unwittingly acquired as passengers in the depths of the forest. He would receive a more thorough examination later under the scrutiny of his mate, but for now it is a time of rejoicing and celebration.

The people of his village loved Yarpay, not only for his skill as a hunter and provider, but for his talent as a storyteller and collector of myths and legends. He un-shouldered a satchel filled with sweet berries that he deprived from a band of marauding peccaries and some oddly pungent tree nuts that he found in the midst of a squawking brood of garnet Toucans. Without hesitation, the villagers devoured the delicious treats, staining their lips and fingers with the inky red juice of the ripened fruit.

Yarpay's clan is a delightfully innocent people. They are gentle and playful, and act unselfconsciously without prepossession. Their actions are honest and direct. They conceal nothing. Their emotions are not redirected or sublimated. Every passion, every torment is experienced in the moment. Their feelings are not deflected or re-channeled along an emotional causeway or impounded as a reservoir for future action. They eat when they are hungry, they lie down when tired. They shout when they are angry. They scream when they are frightened. This condition of feral innocence would soon change, however.

An accidental hypertrophy in the hippocampus of Yarpay, which allowed him to store his experiences as memory, would be passed on to his descendants. The power of memory would be highly adaptive, and his heirs would reap the rewards, outcompeting every other lineage.

Yet, memory is a heavy appendage. It is a powerful weapon and unwieldy device that makes its user formidable but is also a terrible burden to carry. Not unlike the fearful cannons pulled miserably through fields of mud and lowered from cliffs into steep ravines, the cast iron and bronze falconets deployed by the Conquistadors in their decisive campaign against the Aztec people were fearsome weapons, but the cost of slogging through enemy terrain with the awful tonnage made their army slow and ponderous, compared to the agility and rapid maneuvering of his foes.

Similarly, Yarpay's people were a lithe and quick-witted people, who lived in the moment. Unburdened by thoughts of the past, or calculations of an imagined future, they were immersed in the splendor of being alive.

The development of memory was the end of innocence. It was the deep well of remembrance that drowned the whole world in anguish. Human memory is the fountain of the deep, and just as the Yarpayans had the capacity to store long term memories, the tribal reservoir of recrimination and retribution began filling with a large ocean of resentment.

The mosaic flood existed, but it was not physical, it was existential. The deluge of things that could not be forgotten or forgiven, that was the apocalypse. Two by two, the beasts of memory were weighed and counted. Two by two, the base pairs of human recorded history were implanted in the arc of memory. Two by two, the heritage of an ancient people entwined in a spinning golden thread.

Yarpay selected a large chunk of magnesium crystal and tossed it into the fire. The crystal ignited with ferocity, casting sparks and flame high into the night air. He stood with his back to the intense heat of the fire animating dark shadows that moved like a terrible raiding party throughout the encampment.

He raised his hands, calling for silence. He is desperate to share what he has learned. In gratitude and humility, he praises the forest. On this day, the forest in its wisdom taught him something new, and in its love for his people, the forest has allowed him to share this new knowledge.

Yarpay explains that the fire that inscribes the shadows that walk around the campfire at night also exists in him. There is a fire that burns within that is no less bright than the ship of the sun in its journey across the sky. The fire within casts shadows, not of darkness but of shimmering light. He tells them that everyone must share this shadow, and when they are awake, it guides them, and when they are asleep it protects them and watches over them. When we sing and dance, we are dancing the dream of another.

Zev Bronski

CHAPTER 6 – MESSAGE IN A BOTTLE

C ast onto the oceans of time by a prehistoric Robinson Crusoe, the message bobbed innocently on the warm currents of human physiology for a half million years until it was plucked from oblivion by John's genetic analysis. He now found himself thrust into an unlikely union with a strange, but obviously talented, young geneticist who impressed him for his deep insights. "Can I trust him?" he thought as he watched Silas work the computer diligently.

"I thought so," Silas said conclusively. "These very dense, compact regions of code are actually plant DNA, just as I had surmised."

"Plant DNA? What's that doing in there? Human and plant DNA parted ways over a million years ago."

He pointed to the screen. "Look at these plant and human sequences. They are like a hand in a glove."

"Strange." John scratched his head. "I've never seen anything like this before."

"I'm not sure I'm going to be able to retrieve the code without the complete genomic sequence of this plant, whatever it is. It's like trying to get bubble gum out of someone's hair."

"Can we isolate it and cross-reference to a plant

~30~

library? If we can pull together some of the banner sequences, maybe we can get enough for a profile and do some subtractive sequencing."

Silas was pleased with John's suggestion. Regaining his pace, Silas quickly assembled a partial "strawman" profile that would allow them to access the Svalbard Global Seed Index. Silas introduced his *strawman* into the search engine and then unconsciously held his breath, waiting for the result...then:

No known match.

"Darn. I thought we had something," Silas said, his voice laced with frustration.

"Did you really think it was going to be that easy?" John was about to begin one of his rants about the younger generation and technology-assisted immediate gratification, but then thought better of it. No sense rubbing salt in the wound. "Look, this is ancient material, and likely extinct. Or if it's not extinct, it may be exceedingly rare. Rare enough that it hasn't been collected, or perhaps it hasn't even been seen before. That's why I never trust the proxy data unless I've made the observations myself. There are too many problems with contaminated samples, unpaid student assistants doing the groundwork, methodological shortcuts...you name it. So, here is what we're going to do. We're going to compare this thing to...let's say the top fifteen closest species and see what we get."

Now John worked the computer while Silas watched over his shoulder.

"You see, here's a potential match. It looks like there's a related species of plant that turned up on the Botanical Medicine Encyclopedia in 1981. There are no subsequent references. It drops off the map at that point. Either that plant went extinct, or no one has bothered to harvest any specimens since then. Let's see here...hmm...interesting. The plant seems to have been confined to a very narrow set of geospatial coordinates. According to this, your plant has some aunts and uncles in Guatemala."

Silas was beginning to enjoy this new collaboration. As John warmed up to him, he felt like he was playing with a good doubles partner.

"Pretty remote...it looks like...uninhabited jungle. But I wonder..." John was thinking aloud once again, then: "If this material is as inextricable from human DNA as it appears to be, that tells me there is a long tradition of historic association, don't you think?"

Silas wasn't sure if John was asking him directly, or if he was talking to himself again, so he responded with an awkward, "Yes, I think that must be correct."

Silas continued looking over John's shoulder as he issued commands into a navigational compass for a positioning satellite. "What are you doing?"

"You remember the bear piss stuff I used to do for the Outer Reach Corporation?"

Silas was feeling embarrassed by his earlier

remark.

"I still retain some of my privileges to their satellite network. I'm redirecting one of their multispectral imaging satellites to scan the region where your plant relative was discovered."

"They let you do that?" Silas seemed surprised.

"Well, sort of...I mean, who's keeping track anyway?" John winked mischievously.

The laser scanned across the landscape, revealing a dense network of roads, bridges, canals, and buildings that had lain hidden beneath the vault of the upper tree canopy for centuries. A detailed map of the city emerged on John's screen with three dimensional elevations highlighted in red, green, and yellow to differentiate manmade from natural topographic features.

"Simple as that." John hit the print button on his 3D printer, and the Cartesian gantry began racing across the printer platform like a machine possessed. Layer by layer, the ancient city rose from its massive foundations. In only a few moments, the printer had duplicated in miniature the Herculean efforts of perhaps ten generations of people who had quarried the limestone blocks, cut and fitted the joints together with such precision that the project would leave modern engineers utterly baffled at how such a feat could ever have been accomplished.

Still, the 3D extruder nozzle persisted, unaware of the improbable existence of the city it was steadily replicating. Higher and higher it grew, deftly climbing the near vertical step pyramids where priests and kings once scaled their dizzying heights to shouts of praise and exaltation.

At last, the nozzle culminated at the jaguar-faced cornice that adorned the central temple. The visage of the fierce predator that looked out upon the city was both human and feline in its countenance. The murderous fangs and whiskers were betrayed by oddly human looking eyes.

John stifled the impulse to make his thought known. "Did the anthropomorphic tendency of the ancient artist to inspirit all animals with a human soul inform his creation, or was it a literal translation?"

He gazed at the city that must have inspired its citizens with a sense of awe for the works of their ancestors. He realized that he had been living in a world that had summarily disposed of the wisdom of the ancients. A few myths and legends, a hieroglyph or frieze panel was all that remained. What did we actually know about these people and the way they lived? He had foolishly assumed that modern man stood mightily on the precipice of history. How many civilizations had come and gone? How many ripples of humanity had broken on the endless shore, expending their energy in the surging whitewash, only to recede again and again into a primeval state of chaos?

John had borrowed adaptive traits from Tolstoy the bear, and the common Wood frog. "Have we been too hasty in disregarding the evidence of human and animal hybrids?" John regarded Silas. "Genoglyphs...indeed." Then turning back toward the model of the lost city, he asked Silas, "Is your international passport updated?" Compared to the startling emergence of the primordial city he had just witnessed, the question seemed strangely incongruous and caught Silas by surprise.

"Passport?"

"You'll need one if we're going to find your plant."

CHAPTER 7 – THE DESCENDANTS

Centuries had passed since Yarpay's fireside revelation to his people. The notion that they were the living dreams or shadow beings of the primary dreamer had made them different. Lost was the former spontaneity of their interactions. They became aware of themselves as unique and disparate conscious entities. They began to ask questions like, "Does the primary dreamer have the same dream of everyone?" "Are some dreams more favored than others?" "If the dreamer forgets someone's dream and they are again remembered, do they return to this world?" "If one hides from the dreamer, how long can one last and will they ever be found?"

The questions erupted in such a profusion that no one could properly agree on all the answers. Some of the great questions had been resolved, but over time were forgotten. Many times, disputes would arise and disagreement as to whether certain knowledge of the dreamer could be apprehended by his dream shadows.

People even began to describe themselves according to their epistemological position on certain key questions such as "Do animals have their own dreamer?" and "Is the dreamer happy with his dreams or is he afraid of them?"

It was at last decided that someone of great knowledge and wisdom should be responsible for questions pertaining to the dreamer. And they would make it their duty to understand the dreamer by asking, "Why does the primary dreamer dream in the first place?" "Is there yet another dreamer beyond the primary dreamer who is also dreamed?" By assigning this task to a single individual, the people could go about their business unconcerned and focus on themselves.

They detached themselves from the responsibility of questioning and laid the wreath of knowing at the one who bites his tongue. This man, who was known to convulse on the ground in fits and spasms, spoke eloquently on the dreamer. After such a paroxysm, he would vomit yellow bile and stare into the fire for hours. Urmachiscan was his name. During his meditations, the people would place cups of spiced honey at his side for nourishment and attach grasshoppers to his head for good luck. The division of moral labor freed them from the anxiety of the sacred myth.

Thus, having dispensed of the vexing mystery of origins, the people turned inward. They adorned their bodies with a rich paint derived from the fat of the wild boar and inscribed splendid arabesques of mercury, flecked with leaves of shimmering gold upon their skin. Their long hair was meticulously braided and fragranced with cloves and cinnamon. They wore elegant finery woven from banana thread and diaphanous spider silk that had been submerged in an array of colors from green coffee leaves, scarlet cactus bugs, orange Osage, and yellow blossoms of the dahlia. Like birds-of-paradise, the Yarpayans moved through their world, milling about as though a loud noise might suddenly cause them to take flight into the heavens.

Jealous of their youth and great beauty, and fearful of what lies beyond the world of dreams, the Yarpayans participated in elaborate rituals of rejuvenation. One of their great ancestors had discovered the key to longevity. It was the healer Kuma who noticed that the vehicle of birth had great life-giving power. She obtained leeches from sea grass in the shallow waters of the black river and placed the leeches upon the placenta and umbilical cord from a new mother of twins. She allowed the leeches to gorge themselves on the fresh blood, which was rich with the tissue of maternal and fetal stem cells. She then placed the leeches on her sick patients. Within weeks the infirm were rehabilitated and the aged had been restored to a more youthful disposition.

Now, with the birth of each new child, the elixir of life held in the placental afterbirth and transmuted through the kindness of the unassuming leech, was celebrated and shared throughout the village. The villagers no longer counted their age in years and decades, but in centuries.

CHAPTER 8 – DEPARTURE

John's dog, a Chesapeake Bay Retriever named Bill, was the spirit of obedience. He was the embodiment of generations of carefully selected breeding that winnowed the highest aspirations of human societies, which seemed only to have lodged with any sense of determination or purpose in the souls of canines. If Chesapeakes had a motto, it would be the envy of every Leatherneck: "Serve or Die."

As he unpacked Bill's travel kit, which contained a variety of blankets, amusements, treats, and toys, he began to feel the hollowness that he always experienced when he was separated from Bill for any length of time. It was some consolation to him that his father would be the foster parent of Bill's affection, but parting was never easy.

"Okay, I think we're all squared away." John arranged Bill's meals in the kitchen cabinet. "This should be enough food and treats for at least a month." John knew that his father would be secretly lavishing Bill with table scraps and perhaps even preparing Bill's favorite dish of chicken fettuccini, but there was no sense in confronting him. He would do what he pleased, and in this situation, John was grateful to have a loving, albeit somewhat irresponsible, caretaker.

"Where did you say you're going?" John's father asked absentmindedly.

"Dad, I have my entire itinerary right here on this sheet. I'll be in Guatemala. You probably won't be able to get in contact with me once I'm there, but there is a list of emergency numbers on the counter that you can call, including Bill's veterinarian."

"Guatemala, you say, oh good...I hope you have a fine time."

John was content to let his father believe that he was going on vacation. Their conversations tended to revolve around neutral subjects that didn't arouse disagreement. His father viewed vestigial phenotype rescue with thinly veiled suspicion. He believed that the world exists as it is today for a reason. Although he couldn't specifically assign purpose to such unseemly contrivances like the Duck-billed platypus, in his heart he felt that it was simply better to leave well-enough alone.

John's parents had lived through a pandemic that destroyed their business and resulted in their eventual separation. The global disease was the bastard child of high-minded individuals tinkering in matters they didn't understand and could not possibly comprehend. A collusion of technocrats and dilettantes convinced of their own moral correctness, viewing themselves as the proper custodians of a scientific technique that was gifted to them like a box of Christmas pears from their intellectual superiors.

To his dad, the disease was a plague of the elites forced upon the masses. And once the virus had completed its gruesome errand, the petty Hitlers, who populate and infest the corridors of every civic institution, seized on the opportunity to fashion the iron manacles of authoritarianism. Even his father's beloved Australia fell victim to the madness and hysteria, imprisoning its citizens in concentration camps with the drooling complicity of its frightened people. The manmade disease would eventually evolve into a less pathogenic species, but the independence of the people and their freedom was never returned to them. "Once the wolf has tasted the blood of your sheep it must be destroyed," John's father had told him.

Laden attempted to win his father's approval, or at least assuage his fears, by reminiscing on one of his favorite stories. "Dad," he had interrupted with a note of constrained hope in his voice, but his father was only partially aware of him and didn't notice his son's intervention. Little by little his father was forging ahead into a new world of waking dreams populated with apparitions of the past. The ghosts of old friends came and went, his deceased older brother would stop by on his way to the racetrack, offering to press a bet, and occasionally a young version of his mother as he once remembered her from childhood, would rest her weary feet on his ottoman after gathering the morning's laundry. His memory, which was filled with experience, was now running in reverse. The voices and faces that had been imprinted in his mind over a lifetime was spilling over, projecting phantoms into the physical world. John was careful so as not to invade the delicate trance that occupied his father. A presence too sudden could startle his father, causing a painful re-emergence not unlike the bubbles of nitrogen that violate the blood of a scuba diver who had breached the surface during a rapid ascent.

John noticed how Bill's affection had focused his father's attention and kept him grounded in reality. Weeks ago he made up his mind to give Bill to his father, but he was in no rush to surrender his best friend. "We'll have that conversation when I return."

"Dad, I have to go soon."

His father regarded him with pleasure and asked him to sit. The two men sat quietly and simply enjoyed each other's proximity while Bill circled a warm patch of sun and then made his final approach, landing comfortably on the Persian rug.

After everything had been said, it was not quips and jabs, or even fanciful tales, but a silent devotion of two people traveling along similar destinies and sharing a common respect that joined them in the world. Like two friends on a road trip, enjoying the scenery, they just sat together, soaking in the ambient silence.

"That was really something, who could have imagined..." His father's words trailed off, as he was again lost in reverie.

Palinode – "Keeper of Legends"

John saw his opportunity and offered, "Dad, do you remember the Landcruiser?"

There was a brief sparkle in his father's eyes accompanied by a mischievous grin. He scratched the top of his head and adjusted himself in his seat. "Oh, you must be talking about the FJ40." John's father had returned to earth, and with the red meat of his Landcruiser to chew on, John now had his full attention.

"Yes, the FJ, that's right, dad. Do remember what you told me...about how you found it?"

The story of his discovery was one of his favorites and had been often repeated over the years. The yarn would change with minor alterations to suit his audience, but he never got bored telling the story, and he slid into the narrative like putting on a pair of warm socks. He chuckled, "That old timer. Who would have thought he had such a treasure?"

John's father was one of the last of a dying breed. He had received his veterinary license from the state agricultural college and spent much of his career traveling to and from the various cattle ranches, dairy farms, and equestrian stables in the county. He had hoped that his son might follow him into the business, but it was not to be.

"In those days we didn't mind bartering for our lunch," he said. "You see, this farmer had run up quite a bill. Why am I telling you this story anyway? You've heard it before."

"I like to hear you tell it."

His father didn't need any further encouragement and continued dutifully. "The thing is that, when you get out into the rural areas, it's like traveling back in time. People are self-sufficient, you know. You can't just run down to the store for all your needs. If you want something, you've either got to make it, or borrow it, or trade for it. That's what I liked about working with those folks. They were talented in so many ways...very innovative in their approach to solving the problems associated with mundane tasks. And when you make something with your own hands, there's a real feeling of accomplishment that you don't get any other way. We're a tool-making species by nature, but we've been reduced to scavengers. Who wants to be a jackal or a baboon?

"In the same way, when you work the land, and especially when you are close to the animals, you develop a very commonsense approach to life. Someone once asked me how I would define intelligence. I told him, "It's obvious. Intelligence means you have a clear sense of priority." Too many people get caught up in things that just don't add up in the long run. Anyhow, I had been providing veterinary care for this farmer, and to some extent I had been treating his family, as well. Medical doctors were in short supply, and after all, people are great apes, so I was more than happy to oblige.

"One day, I'm checking in with this farmer, and

you know I never was particularly good at the collections part of the business. When someone hasn't paid in a while, I know they're hurting, so it becomes uncomfortable. But this farmer pulls me aside and says he wants to show me something. I follow him to an old woodshed behind the barn, and it's crammed with junk. Unbelievable, this guy kept everything. Road signs, bear traps, oil cans, a stuffed coyote. I can't imagine why anyone would go to the trouble of stuffing a coyote, but there it was in all its majesty, frozen in mid-stride. I'm thinking to myself, "Is this it? He wants me to see his coyote?" But he squeezes past the mangy trophy and continues past a Pall Mall vending machine and an old Getty fuel pump, where my attention is directed to a vehicle that has been covered under a large canvass tarp. He starts rolling the tarp from the front bumper, and I get a glimpse of the emblem on the grill, and I can't believe what I'm witnessing. As he carefully removes the tarp from the hood of the car, I'm thinking this is the best striptease I've ever seen...a 1967 Spring Green FJ40 in mint condition appears from beneath the cover. The farmer, who had been concerned with folding the tarp, turned around and caught my expression of astonishment and smiled. "I thought you might get a kick out of this. I can always tell when someone has the car bug.

"I was struggling to comprehend how it got there, and how long had it been there, and why? I found myself stammering, "But, I've never seen you drive it.

What's it doing back here?"

The old farmer grinned. "When my brother passed on, I was left with his vehicle. I knew how much it meant to him, and for some reason I couldn't bring myself to drive it, but I couldn't just get rid of it either. So here it sits.

"I felt privileged that he was willing to share this painful memory with me and give me a private exhibition of his most prized possession. I was giddy like a little kid. "Can I look at the interior?" "Of course. Slide into the driver's seat and see how it feels."

"The farmer had taken meticulous care of the FJ, and as I climbed into the cabin, I could smell the well-oiled leather, a fragrance of sweet almond oil and beeswax. As I gripped the wheel and placed my hand over the gear selector, I thought to myself, there are times when engineering and aesthetics meld together perfectly. An effective design always looks good for some reason. It's like, instinctually, we just know when something works.

"Then I suddenly realized I had been daydreaming as I sat in the front seat. Embarrassed, I removed myself from the cabin and retreated into the chaos of the shed. "What do you think?" the farmer asked, carefully studying my expression. "It's fantastic. Thank you for sharing this with me. It is truly a work of art." "I'm glad to hear you say that" the farmer replied, "because it's yours."

"I'm not sure how long I stood there staring at the

man, but after I recovered my sense of composure, I began to apologize and insist that I couldn't accept such an extraordinary gift. "Nope. My mind is made up. It's yours. Besides, it's not just about you. You need some reliable transportation, and I'm not the only one who needs you. My neighbors need you too. So, if it makes you feel any better about it, this is my gift to the entire community."

"Dumbfounded, I accepted the keys and drove the FJ down the dirt access road of the farmstead and out onto the highway. It had been quite some time since the vehicle had been tuned, and the carburetor was running rich, filling the cabin with the pungent smell of gasoline, causing my pupils to burn. As I raced down the two-lane county road, the world took on a dreamy aspect under the influence of the carbon monoxide fumes. The satisfying hum of the FJ's tires vibrating upward through the suspension and into the floorboards sounded like the gentle roll of a kettle drum as a prelude to some unfinished symphony. I leaned heavily on the accelerator and chased the setting sun across the furrowed valley as it withdrew from the expanse of sugar beets and cabbage into the low foothills, and made its escape, finally, into the welcoming arms of dusk. If you're lucky, you might have a half-dozen or so perfect days in your life. That was one of mine."

John was surprised and a little taken aback by his last comment. It seemed lately that his father had been taking stock of his life's experience and filing those memories into a kind of existential inventory of days, assigning an appropriate level of significance to each recollection. John wondered how much of life's lessons are recorded and imprinted in the genome, and whether this deliberative process of categorizing good and bad experiences that seemed to occupy his father, was an outward manifestation of instinct formation and preservation that was happening at a much deeper level in his father's biology.

He was familiar with the notion of strange attractors, otherwise known as fractals, and how complex organic structures like the leaves on a tree are the result of a set of simple repeating microstructures. "Does it happen in reverse?" he thought. Perhaps the chaotic pattern of exuberance associated with a moonlit joyride is distilled into rudimentary instructions, spun down to their crystalline essence, where they impregnate in the genetic spine.

"Dad, I wanted you to be the first person to know. I've finally done it. I found my hidden treasure."

John's father raised his head and carefully studied his son's expression. He had seen that look in his son's eyes before, a long time ago, but in recent years the glimmer of enthusiasm had gone away and was replaced with a kind of dull resignation. For a moment, that young boy who would breathlessly retell the story of his day's misadventures, was suddenly returned and standing before him.

"Where did you go?" his father asked sadly.

Palinode – "Keeper of Legends"

"I didn't go anywhere, dad. I'm here beside you. I just wanted you to know...I wanted you to know that things turned out all right for me. You don't have to worry anymore. From now on it's going to be better."

CHAPTER 9 – SHANGRI-LA

A thousand years had passed since Urmachiscan completed his journey, and his noble dream was welcomed into the earth. The Yarpayans had moved from the forest onto the fertile plain where they sowed maize in the rich soil. Swirled terraces of purple amaranth climbed the foothills like the fingerprints of a giant with palms held supine, a mendicant with bowed head, awaiting the monsoon rain from a benevolent sky. The floodwaters were conscripted and forced into channels that fed irrigation troughs radiating throughout the city, bringing a cool breeze to the public plaza, and fighting back the midday sun with languid reflecting pools that imitated the sincerity of the city's inhabitants.

The gleaming walls of the city were composed of layers of polished limestone and basalt honed to perfection with diamond rasps and an emulsion of coconut oil and buttermilk. The towering edifice was embedded with dazzling bits of fire opal, fossil brachiopods, and marine snails captured in time, their bodies now initiated into the fortress wall, which was an unlikely reimagining of their hard protective shell, making the soft human inhabitants a kind of land-going mollusk in a reef of massive quarried stones. Blocks of volcanic obsidian pulled indifferently by sled teams of camels from the highlands and heaved onto river barges were dramatically arranged as capstones along the fortress parapet.

The master architect, Toltec, supervised the placement of every stone, every monolith, caisson, and well. As he observed the stone mason placing his cut line, he lost himself in speculation. "If the mason's chisel were perfectly sharp, could it be stopped from cutting? And if such an ideally sharpened tool were dropped by the stone mason, would the blade not continue to cut through the earth, breaking and separating stone and soil until what? Is there an immutable substance that cannot be cut where the blade would, at last, come to a rest? Or would it continue unabated, slicing and ripping its way to the center of the earth as the soil closed in behind it?"

Increasingly, Toltec had been given to such flights of fancy during his workday. He strived to understand how organizing the movement of people could improve the social life of the city. The primitive communal existence of the Yarpayans was but a distant dream at this stage. The Yarpayans had become stratified according to wealth and position. Toltec's job was to isolate and quarantine certain elements of the population while allowing for public discourse. He created spaces of the sacred and the profane, places for games and for ritual.

Subdivided by intrinsic nature and deliberate intention, Toltec understood that he was organizing the bodies of people into segments of moral worth.

Toltec was an early student of human physiology. He understood the function of the circulatory system and the various tissues and organ systems that comprised the human body. As a young foot soldier, he had treated the festering wounds of his comrades and washed the broken bodies of the fallen. He had witnessed a failing heart work to its last contraction as it hemorrhaged blood from a lacerated artery into the thirsty soil and saw how a sucking chest wound could be sealed with tree sap glue and a banana leaf.

He sought to impress this knowledge of human anatomy in the proper design of his city in building the subterranean bowels of the sewerage system, the pulsing and beating heart of the market plaza, the discerning judge of civic jurisprudence lodged in the forum, the ethereal breath of the temple of shadows, and the bludgeoning fists of the military garrison. The centerpiece of the city was a single fir tree to signify Yarpay's day of understanding.

Still considering his paradox of the ideal blade, he walked through the busy streets crowded with merchants and street vendors. He occasionally stopped to talk to a fish monger or wine peddler, exchanging friendly greetings and sharing the news of the day. The marketplace was a cacophony of caged monkeys, wild dogs, and shouting auctioneers. Nubile virgins, or so they attested, danced erotically to the sound of copper anklet bells and a group of throat singers aroused their delight.

The street bizarre was alive with the sights and smells of baskets of salted piranha, live crawfish, and smoked electric eels, red and purple sautéed chilies, sweet onions, marinated plums and dried fruit, spiced plantains, stewed meat of every contrivance from varmint to hoofed and toed ungulate, clay jars of roasted beetles and plump mealworms, sizzling cakes of fried lemon and honeypot ants, toasted bee larvae, and pickled Dodo eggs, and these were just a few of the offerings on display.

On festival days, the general tumult would rise to a chaotic frenzy as highlanders from afar invaded the city, bringing trade goods and livestock that were strange and exotic to the city dwellers. Creatures that were oddly familiar yet somehow counterfeit, displaying the curious adaptations of the northern latitudes; horned, spiked, bedeviled, and most of all delicious.

One such vendor caught the attention of Toltec as he paused to admire the man's display. Draped across the table was a yellow brocade with the image of a red agaric mushroom being eaten by a green tree frog, who is in turn partially consumed by a poisonous viper. The curious scene was superimposed on an indigo field of jeweled six-point stars. "Nature's apothecaries," the man said wryly as he arranged his inventory of medicaments. "They've been doing this longer than we have."

Toltec studied the impressive variety of poultices, powders and potions, ointments and lineaments of varying degrees of potency from hypnotic and trance-inducing, to somnorifics, violent purgatives and deadly poisons.

"What are we peddling today, kind sir, soporific dreams of ecstasy, forgetfulness and freedom from conscience, a young man's libido, an old man's wisdom, unearned confidence, cures for boredom, perhaps?

"Yes, of course. That and so much more." The apothecary smiled graciously. "Something far greater. Self-knowledge. What would a man such as yourself pay to know his own motivations? If you could all at once, strip away your pretensions, would you? Would you stand bare in the nakedness of your honest self, exposed to your memories?"

Toltec was taken aback by the man's improvidence. They had never met. Toltec was a man of the ruling elite, and this itinerant merchant presumed to know, or at least pretended to understand, his inner torment. "Excuse me, sir, but I believe you may have the best of me. Do we know each other?" Toltec let the merchant know that he had overstepped his bounds.

"Why no. I just imagined that you are someone with whom I can speak directly, without coercion or inducement. You strike me as the kind of man who speaks plainly and expects such in return."

Toltec felt abandoned by his initial anger and gave into his natural curiosity. "What is this you say about knowing my motivations? Certainly, every man knows his own mind. How could he not?"

"Sir. I am but a simple peddler. My experience of this world is limited to this apothecary stand and the few tonics that I offer as a comfort to people who are in pain. But I assure you that the effort that people exert in refusing self-awareness and removing all knowledge of their passage in this world is equivalent to the exertions that built the very foundations of this city."

The apothecary advised him of a powerful plant extract that would allow him to see the record of his own life and memories in a rich cascade, a procession of remembrance that would dance and sing just like the celebrants who came to circumambulate the great fir tree. He promised that the experience would lighten the weight of his brow and give him a renewed sense of purpose, if only he had the courage to try.

CHAPTER 10 – THE SOURCE

Silas was nervous as the small amphibious plane made its descent. The pilot banked aggressively, and Silas was pushed deep into his seat, reminding him of the astonishing moment when it was revealed to him that entropy and gravity were one and the same.

The craft was gently buffeted by the upwelling thermals that lifted swarms of mosquitoes and fruit flies to soar high into the clouds where the trade winds would take them even higher into the upper atmosphere and beyond, into space where they drifted among satellites and huddled like refugees in the Lagrange points, miniature arthronauts who boldly flew where no human had flown before.

The pilot was weaving confidently through thunder bursts and dense columns of rain, dipping and dodging like a skilled boxer evading the jabs of a more powerful, but somewhat clumsy punch-drunk palooka.

The forest canopy looked like a cross section of green fluorescent gel-stained brain tissue, and it made Silas think about the Gaia folks who believed the forest had a collective hive-mind. From this altitude, he might well believe it. The twisted, knotted chaos of vines and branches that choked out the light and plunged erratically into the spongy matte of desiccating leaves, seemed an impregnable fortress at ground level. Yet, from the exalted position of the feisty De Havilland DHC-2 Beaver, the uncompromising logic of the forest network was resolved.

John looked over at his compatriot, who was by now afflicted with a profound disagreement between his head and his stomach, smiled comfortingly. "Don't worry, as soon as we're on the ground you'll feel much better."

The pilot looked back at Silas with a mildly concerned expression as if to say, "Don't make a mess on my upholstery."

An old familiar friend and constant companion of the Guatemalan sky since it arrived from Canada in the early 1980s to explore potential oil reserves, the De Havilland had joined the million-mile club over ten years ago, and its sturdy air frame continued to shuttle people and supplies throughout Petén.

The trusty De Havilland and its pilot were neutral regarding all things legal, political, and religious, but resolutely orthodox in their passion for bush flying. An unscheduled flight from Nicaragua to Mexico once carried Pablo Escobar and 50 kilos of cocaine, and the return leg transported a crew of Jesuit Missionaries and their supply of donation bibles, each personally inscribed by the Archbishop of Mexico City. The final stage of the trip arrived in Honduras to deposit a scrum of would-be Marxist revolutionaries and a wooden crate of Russian-made AK-47s of Vietnam War vintage. Whether medical supplies, contraband, or drums of Agent Orange, the pilot had a strict "no questions asked" policy, and John and Silas felt no compunction to break with tradition.

The pilot searched for a familiar gaping wound in the fleshy nether regions of the Petén Forest where he could make his aeronautical transfusion into the venous flow of the Ixcan river. After he spotted the point of entry, he rolled the De Havilland gently and descended through the mist onto the river's turgid surface, which was swollen from the recent downpour. As the pontoons slid along the surface, the water boiled with a school of cichlids. One of the fish leaped through the rear sliding window of the plane and landed in Silas's lap. Surprised by the sudden appearance of the stowaway, the three men laughed, and Silas threw the fish back into the river, then wiped scales from his hands with a handkerchief.

Deftly throttling the Pratt & Whitney radial engine, the pilot managed to advance another half-mile up the river, fighting the current and carefully navigating the pontoons around an obstacle course of submerged logs, sand bars, and floating debris. At last, the plane arrived at a small landing that projected from the muddy shore, a pier constructed of simple wooden planks that had been fastened together with braided manila rope and finished with two rusty cleats bolted to the end. The plane glided easily to the boat dock where the pilot expertly lassoed one of the cleats, and then allowed the tail section of the plane to rotate with the current until he could hop out and knot the second dock line.

John and Silas unloaded their gear.

"I'll return in two weeks," the pilot said, who had other customers to contend with. "You'll be in good hands, don't worry. I have arranged for Airto to take you to your destination. He is an excellent tracker and knows as much about the forest as anyone in this part of Petén. He's good company and I know you will enjoy listening to his stories."

"How do we let him know we have arrived?" John asked.

"I'm sure he already knows. He would have heard the engine and seen us circling. Just make yourself comfortable and be patient."

Comfort seemed out of the question, but this was the second time during this trip that a local had to remind them to be patient. Time moved glacially here.

The gears of the equatorial sundial turned at a leisurely pace, and the incessant clicking of insects needed a drop of watchmaker's oil. A coatimundi perched high overhead yawned dreamily to the metronomic swaying of its favorite rubber tree.

"What do we do now?" Silas was now recovered from his earlier motion sickness.

John looked around helplessly, while trying to

convey an attitude of calm authority. "Yes, well, this is what we will do. We will construct a fire ring over here. That way our river guide, Mr. Airto will see the smoke and realize that we have arrived."

"The pilot said he would know we were here by the sound of the plane's engine." Silas saw no benefit in John's seemingly redundant gesture.

John was quietly annoyed by Silas's opposition. He was out of his element, and after being deposited in the middle of the jungle, his anxiety was growing. He needed a project to occupy his limbic system, so he pathetically started gathering rocks for his fire ring despite Silas's lack of enthusiasm.

Shamed into action by John's solitary effort, Silas grudgingly began collecting rocks and consciously arranged them in a circular pattern, although any configuration would have well sufficed. "Why always a circle?" he thought. "Surely a square or triangle would achieve the same purpose." No matter. He continued arranging his default Boy Scout firepit and then noticed they had a visitor.

Stepping from behind a tree as if he had left for only a moment to put another tray of cinnamon rolls in the oven, Airto emerged from the forest and made his way to the landing.

Airto moved with a quickness of step that belied his many years. As he walked along the shoreline, waving to his new friends, John could read the emblem on his shirt, "Cincinnati Bengals LVI Super Bowl

Champions." For an instant, John thought he had slipped into a strange parallel universe where the Bengals didn't suck. Then he realized this was one of the many pre-printed losing team jerseys that got boxed-up after a defeat and were sent to faraway lands where people could participate in the vicarious joys of a championship season that wasn't to be. He wondered if the river guide had ever heard of Joe Burrow. "Probably not," he considered, "but it's a nifty shirt, and the guy looks good in the black and orange colors of his adopted team."

Around his neck hung a thin beaded necklace with a kind of totem dangling against his chest. A talisman or good luck charm perhaps? As Airto drew near, John could see that the totem was nothing more than a corkscrew and bottle top opener. John grinned at his own naiveté. He had been in the forest for approximately twenty minutes, and he was already manifesting childlike fantasies of medicine men and their potent earth magic.

Fitted on Airto's head was a smart-looking Tyrolean hat with a brightly colored quetzal feather inserted on one side of the rope band. John, for the moment, wished that he were a hat person, but short of cold weather gear, he felt that hats were an article of clothing that was unsuitable to his peculiar dimensions, emphasizing the enormity of his cranium. "Too bad," he thought regretfully. His grandfather had always worn a hat that gave him an air of sophistication. "Not for me."

"I am told you are seeking a plant," Airto said. "Not gold, not rare earth metals, not oil or gas, but a plant?" He tweaked his bushy brows quizzically. "What is this plant and why do you think it's here in the Petén?"

John was aware that Airto, and forest guides like him, had been exploited in the past by those in the pursuit of mineral riches, and now the locals were cautious about sharing their secrets. "About three decades ago, a group of biologists from the International Biomedicines Research Group performed a survey of this region. They sampled the genetic material of plants from this area and collected seeds, which they delivered to a seed bank in Norway, along with the latitude and longitude coordinates for each specimen. We discovered that one of the species they collected, although not identical, has a marked similarity to a plant that has become relevant to our genetic research. We believe that if we can find this plant, it will be the key to solving our genetic puzzle, that is, if it's not extinct."

"I see." Airto nodded. "This forest keeps many secrets. And what is this great mystery that compels the two of you to come to Petén? What is it that you hope to find at the end of your journey?"

Silas, who as the junior partner of the endeavor had been deferring to John up to this point, could no longer bite his tongue and decided to assert himself.

Palinode – "Keeper of Legends"

"We think there's a hidden message that was placed in our bodies by an ancient people of this land. We believe this plant holds the key to unlocking that message."

Airto's curiosity was appeased by the revelation. Justifiably skeptical of the motivations of outsiders who come looking for riches, he believed the pursuit of knowledge was a lofty goal. He remembered the time from his youth when he was introduced by his father to Hernan Cortes. His father believed that the arrival of Cortes on the Caribbean shores was a good omen, and harbinger of great things, since he had arrived from the direction of the rising sun at the beginning of a 52-year cycle of the calendar.

Silas's confession was the demonstration of trust that Airto was searching for. He tenderly placed his hand on Silas's shoulder. "The plant which you seek is called the Keeper of Legends. You are wise to have come here, for its location is not far off. I will help you find it. You will be in my protection, and your questions will be answered."

CHAPTER 11 - BLASPHEMER

After completing his morning errands and administering to the poorest of the city's outlanders, who begged and groveled in the approved spaces, Banik took an interest in a crowd that had spontaneously gathered near the auction platform. There, a man who was strange to him but had the appearance of someone familiar was rallying a group of unhappy revelers to a cause that Banik could not yet understand. The man's high-pitched voice and forceful gestures aroused the excitement of the assembly who pressed inward in a circumference around the podium.

"We are not beholden to history," he proclaimed. "We are not dogs on a leash to be paraded about by the vainglorious notions of a dead past. What wisdom did the ancient ones profess that even a humble school child doesn't learn in his primary letters?"

Banik was aghast at the impudence of the speaker. It was a direct assault on all he had lived for. Through the intervention of the Keeper of Legends, he had shared the dream visions of the elders to help his brethren understand that they were not alone in the world. Though finite in their own mortality, he believed that everyone was eternal in that they shared a continuity with the ancient lives who appeared to them in the ritual. Why would he say such things? More shocking was the quiet applause that rewarded the speaker's words.

"Do they not understand what he is saying?"

Violating his Order's prohibition against public displays of disagreement or involvement in political disputes, Banik raised his voice. "I say to you, sir, why have you come here, and in this place of friendship, reviled the wisdom of the ancients to whom we all owe our gratitude and deepest respect?"

The speaker turned to see Banik standing barefoot in the crowd. "I should have thought so. If it isn't the very one himself, a penitent." He sneered. Then he pointed his finger accusingly at Banik as though he were inviting the derision of the assembly. "You think you are better than all of us, and don't you try to deny it. You derive your power from communion in the ritual, and yet you don't share its secrets. You keep the sacred knowledge that is our birthright hidden. We demand to know what magic is used in the invocation of the fathers."

Banik wasn't expecting this. He could feel the mood of the crowd beginning to turn against him as they were being rallied to the speaker's cause.

"Sir, have you forgotten yourself? The Keeper of Legends was taken under our protection after a terrible calamity, the dimensions of which I shall not speak. It is for the good of all that we confine its use to the ritual.

To do otherwise would be courting disaster." Banik's words, which aimed at striking a conciliatory tone, drew faint nods of approval, but the speaker's bravado was drawing apostates to his fold.

"You see. It's for our protection, he says. Like a mother to a child, or conservator to an idiot. You're not smart enough or have any sense. You can't be trusted. Do you see how they think of us? Simpletons and fools, every one of us." The speaker was clearly gaining momentum and adherents with each new accusation, and the crowd was beginning to stir with an anger that surprised Banik and made him fear for his safety.

"This is what I suggest." The speaker grinned maniacally, gathering energy from the growing crowd. "I say we should go to the temple right now and seize the Keeper of Legends for ourselves. We will be our own priesthood. We will make up our own minds. And we will end the hegemony of the ancient ones."

The announcement was received with shouts and cheers, as the once-peaceful assembly was transformed and departed in willing complicity as an angry mob.

In his moment of triumph, the speaker searched the crowd for the face of his defeated opponent, but Banik had vanished into the entrails of the city.

Only a handful of people were aware of the honeycomb of service corridors that undergirded the city above. The access points had been sealed long ago. Banik's father, who had served as chief engineer in the public improvement's office, once brought Banik into one of the corridors as a young child. An excavation in the basement of a private residence for an unlicensed wine cellar had opened a void in one of the cavern walls, revealing a forgotten aquifer that was populated with a school of miniature blind carp that fed on worms and insects that fell like manna from the broken ceiling. The careful attention of the carp had preserved the aquifer from becoming brackish, and the silent mirror of the water's surface reflected the grandeur of marble arches and tiled mosaics that gratefully adorned the engineering wonder. As his eyes acclimated to the torchlight, he could see his own reflection floating placidly on the silver water. It would be one of the last times he would bear witness to his own face.

The hidden world below the city would be a source of comfort to the child in his developing years. "What mysteries are within reach, perhaps just beneath our feet, but defy our perception?" he would think as he imagined the subtle architecture of a world braced and buttressed by invisible columns, pointed arches, and ribbed vaults that held the burgeoning weight of his waking senses. He was grateful indeed, and when he witnessed the temple, he felt an affinity with its builder, Toltec, who could not have hoped of seeing its completion, but was satisfied that his descendants would gather under its roof one day, and be embraced by his creation long after his death, the donation of an entire lifetime for people he would never know.

Ankle deep in freezing water, Banik groped his

way along the underground passage with arms outstretched, desperately clawing at the darkness. A school of tiny carp nibbled at his feet and tickled his toes. The brick-and-mortar wall that he had been clinging to suddenly transitioned into the polished tiles of an antechamber. His fingertips traced the outline of scrollwork that was familiar to him.

"I'm close."

Within moments, Banik had reached the base of a spiral staircase that ascended to a secret vault behind the temple altar. In previous times, the attendants of the Keeper were given to entertaining their female parishioners in the hidden chamber. The stairwell was abundant with obscene graffiti depicting anthropomorphic phalluses and ungenerous sex acts, as well as some oddly contrived chimeras of half-man, half-beast aggressively engaged in procreative exertions, a twisting scoreboard of youth defiled. What began in private as a whimsical dalliance among young lovers, eroded into a sinister exchange of physical favors for moral enlightenment, which resulted in the unhappy priesthood of eunuchs, like Banik himself, who now presided over the ritual. An innocent victim of carnal pleasures unknown.

Banik emerged unseen into the light of the central nave and was relieved to find that the mob had not breached the inner sanctum. "Perhaps they have come to their senses and abandoned this fool's errand."

Before he could let down his guard, a group of

distraught young acolytes approached him with news of the brigands clamoring to dislodge the west gate. The unimaginable had at last happened, and the neophytes searched Banik's astonished expression for answers. After a moment of confused hesitation, he finally regained his composure and asserted himself. "This is no drunken hoard or band of revelers, I assure you. They come here with a terrible purpose at the bidding of a stranger who I encountered in the streets only a short while ago. They wish to unseat the Order and seize the Keeper of Legends for themselves."

The neophytes gasped in horror. Untold thousands of years of memories placed in jeopardy at the whim of a traveling provocateur. The seismic relevance rippled through their understanding, liquefying the stability of the once-solid ground underneath their feet.

"No one is safe," Banik declared. "This radical has exorcised their emotions to a degree that not one of them is entirely in control of his own thoughts. They are cast upon the sea of chaos, and they move with the fierce continuity of the swarm."

Hearing the sickly thud of human bodies pounding their fists, shoulders, and feet against the west gate and the desiccated recoil of splintering and cracking wood as the massive portcullis offered conditions of its surrender, made Banik realize that the time to abandon the temple had come.

"Go to the atrium and gather every plant, every seed pod, and every root you can muster." He was breathless with urgency. "Make your escape through the floor behind the altar. When you emerge from the lower passage in the city, blend in...let no one see your face. They will be searching for you. You must flee from this city and scatter to the wind.

"Go to the north and disperse among the villagers there, but do not reveal your true self. Find your place in the service of your new family and become a model of obedience.

"To the east you will find merchant vessels on the coast, and safe passage to the spice islands across the water. The islanders are leery of our kind and will find your manner peculiar and unfamiliar to them. You must adapt to their ways and harden yourself to their coarse nature, but do not forget who you are.

"To the west and the highlands, we have many friends, and you will be welcomed. Do not abuse their trust. Receive their kindness with humility but do not be tempted by invitations to sit at the head of the table. You are servants, first and foremost, and you must not become a gambit in their machinations, for this has been our downfall.

"The southern frontier is strictly forbidden. There you will not go. The dwellers in those lands are a people defiled. They have cast aside their noble birthright of an erect posture and move on all fours, huddling like beasts in abject squalor. They are scavengers and thieves who are given to depraved madness and have abandoned all notions of virtue.

Palinode – "Keeper of Legends"

Your kindness shall be turned as a weapon to eviscerate you, and your curiosity will be dulled by the bludgeon of vice and hedonistic pursuits. Your natural affinity for mankind will be blunted by jealousy and vengeance. To venture southward will mean the desecration of your soul, followed by the agonizing corruption and death of the body. Heed my words in this matter, lest you find yourself in the belly of the beast. All will be lost."

In that moment, Banik thought of all the words unsaid that he wished he had uttered in the quiet moments before meals or in the multitude of benign tasks that filled the hours.

Instead, he had withheld his approbation, but why? Now he was releasing his charge into the world like eggs to the spawn, and the kind words that might have fortified their armor was unavailable to them. Perhaps he never imagined they would leave, believing the interwoven mesh of validation that people accumulate link by link to do battle with the world was unnecessary.

"It's too late now," he thought, anguished by his carelessness. In his final instruction he spoke to them. "You have served your masters well, and your time here is ended. I thank you, the people of Yarpay thank you, and the generations of Yarpayans who are entrusted to your keep thank you. Now go and never return."

The neophytes scuffled into the hidden passage and descended into the subterranean network of catacombs where they left their temple cloaks in a pile.

Banik did not follow them. He sipped some cool water from the altar and doused the back of his neck, making himself comfortable as though he were expecting an old friend for supper.

Within moments, the uninvited guests arrived, pouring into the chamber from the narthex. They were grinning maniacally and filled with the depraved self-satisfaction of their transgression. They were seeing the temple, not for the first time, but in a new light, as unsanctified and ripe for the plunder. A field of plenty left unprotected from the circling flock of magpies.

One of the rioters caught sight of Banik resting peacefully on a low seat within a niche against the sanctuary wall. There was something disturbing about Banik's incurious expression, and it made him afraid.

"You won't find what you're looking for," Banik said dispassionately. "The neophytes have left, and they have taken the Keeper with them. This building is nothing more than an empty vessel now, and the city that contains this temple is no more than a pile of rock and rubble. The light of Yarpay is retired from this place and your burden is to tell your fellow citizens that it is gone."

Banik rose from his seat and strode toward the central altar. The assembly of rioters and would-be thieves stared at him in amazement, parting as if against their will to allow his passage. He removed the amber glass from the lantern and set it on the floor. He snuffed out the wick with his thumb and forefinger, leaving a small vortex of white smoke that trailed upward and was dissipated into the air that was heavy with incense.

"Why do you judge us?" one of the rioters shouted.

"I am no judge," Banik said indifferently. "I am simply a witness." And with that he departed through the center of the crowd and walked out of his home.

CHAPTER 12 – CRUCIBLES OF TIME

Airto searched through the tangled web of reeds and thick roots that outlined the river's shore. "We will travel by canoe as far as we can go, and then make camp where the water becomes angry...ah, here it is." He pulled the hull of a canoe from an improvised blind on the riverbank. The vessel was fire carved from the trunk of a single ceiba tree and was large enough to accommodate five men, or at least three with their camping gear. John and Silas looked at each other, impressed at Airto's magic trick. What other rabbits were hidden in this man's sleeve?

He climbed in the canoe and held up a long slender object that was bundled in green tarpaulin and tightly bound with two red bungee cords. He removed the bungees and carefully unwrapped a 5-horsepower trolling engine. Airto attached the motor to the transom and gave the pull cord several sharp, violent tugs until the engine sputtered to life. It sounded like a sleepy old man coughing himself awake from a long afternoon nap. He pushed in the choke valve and the two-stroke motor cleared its throat and began humming contentedly.

Airto reached down under the stern seat where he

stored an old Jerry can and uncoiled a small yellow python that had wrapped itself around the handle. "Let's have a little drink, shall we?" He released the snake into the water. "Place your things in the center of the canoe. John will sit up front on the bow, and Silas, you can sit next to me."

Without the convenience of a bilge pump, the men had to bail rainwater from the hull with an old tin cup that they passed back and forth like the world's worst bucket brigade.

"I think that's about as good as it's going to get," John said, conceding defeat to a few errant puddles.

Silas, who was eager to get moving and who had already soaked much of his clothing by accidentally submerging up to his knees on the riverbank, nodded in approval. "It will probably rain soon anyway. No reason to wring the last drop out of this canoe."

With everyone in agreement, the expedition pushed away from the shore and headed out into the gentle current with the small outboard motor proving its worth. The canoe was heavy and riding low in the water. The buoyant remnant of old growth forest pleading its case with the wise old river, was gratefully accepted as its bow unfolded the surface in waves that rolled amiably in long contours toward the shore, and then rebounded, creating an array of diamond-shaped ripples that grew and expanded in the boat's wake.

For the first time in several days of scrambling through crowded airports, being herded like preslaughter livestock onto a network of suffocating commuter flights, and chasing down dusty taxi cabs, which appeared to deliberately evade their customers as part of some twisted game of "screw the tourist", John had the sense that, instead of traveling to somewhere or through some place, he had in effect, arrived.

It had been a long journey from the point when he had locked the front door to his home and turned to board the airport shuttle. Blissfully gliding down the Ixcan, he permitted himself the luxury of enjoying the voluptuous overgrowth of the forest that seemed a celebration of life's remarkable, if not altogether capricious, ingenuity. From the delicate leaves of the upper canopy that harvested the enormous bounty of the nearest dwarf star, the cascade of energy tumbled downward through a menagerie of odd plants to a cacophony of shrieking mammals, spitting reptiles, and stinging insects before submerging into an aquatic panoply of teaming fish species that churned the water as the canoe made its passage. Not a single niche was left unfilled, and not a drop of the sun's precious energy was squandered.

"Perhaps that is my purpose," he thought. "The creation of my mind is to bear witness to this. Floating in this remote forest on a lonely unassuming world, circling resolutely in the outer arm of the Milky Way galaxy. My mind is formed as a mirror of creation. I was evolved to understand the beauty of this world and take pleasure in its magnificence. I am nature's patron."

Palinode – "Keeper of Legends"

Silas released a large belch that suddenly rattled John back to his senses. His cohort had swallowed a bitter concoction of sodium bicarbonate and magnesium hydroxide to sooth his stomach's discomfort, and the explosion of gas left Silas feeling much relieved but somewhat embarrassed by the unintentional announcement.

John laughed as Silas covered his mouth with one hand while pointing over his shoulder in accusatory fashion at Airto, who didn't seem to be paying much attention anyway.

John fell back into his reverie, and in his state of analog romance was lost once again in considering the fragmentation of the energy well, drilling downward and downward from the nematodes through the foraminifera, as they gather around the warmth of the ionic campfire with their tiny cups extended, a Dickensian host begging "Please sir, I want some more."

Restored by his volcanic eruption, Silas began to take notice how the forest was awash in a hyper-density of information; the extraordinary bandwidth communicated not only at ear-splitting frequencies of shrieking monkeys and screeching Macaws, but also at barely perceptible levels of droning insects, which made him wonder about the preponderance of ultrasonic and low frequency sound that must certainly permeate throughout the tropic soundscape.

"It makes perfect sense," he thought. "The

impenetrability of the forest refused all but the most elaborate visual displays, which made the production of sound the most efficient means of communication."

Unlike his compatriot, who was absorbed in the down-conversion of photons into the biomass, Silas was more attuned to the music of the forest. A musician by training with a penchant for flamenco and the rhapsodic melodies of Spanish gypsies, Silas turned his head back and forth, attempting to ascertain the source of the acoustics that penetrated his eardrums and resonated throughout his body.

"Wall of sound, indeed," Silas thought. "Phil Spector's orchestrations are but a plaintive gasp compared to the orchestra of nature."

John perceived the universe as an ocean of radiation, rolling with waves of matter and spinning vortices, lapping against the gravitational breakwater, forming regions of biological domesticity around distant interstellar harbors. Silas, on the other hand, was more inclined to envision a world as discrete packets of ruthless logic fashioned in the incipient cauldron of the early universe and forged by unrelenting hammer blows into a universal code that is transcribed and repeated in every atom, molecule, and complex system. He is the quintessential digital man.

Still, there was a nagging part of his consciousness that proffered a kind of unreasonable dissent to the domino racetrack that animated John's somewhat promiscuous world view.

Palinode – "Keeper of Legends"

He was skeptical of the inevitability of life and often imagined there might be some provision for a hidden inspirational force.

Dragging the tips of his fingers through the water, Silas was unconsciously drawing whirlpools of spectral motion like a kinetic art piece spinning just beneath the surface. High above the forest floor, a Keel-billed toucan unleashed a salvo of squawking that pierced the atmosphere. Was it an invitation? An announcement of ripened fruit or receptivity to procreation? Or a warning perhaps, sounding the alarm of a spotted leopard crouched in anticipation, or a green anaconda preparing its coils like a muscular lasso to ensnare and suffocate its hapless victims.

Silas looked over at Airto who was peacefully captaining the canoe. "He knows...he's been listening to this language his entire life," Silas thought. "Just look at him...smiling like he's listening to an old friend who has told the same yarn a hundred times, but inevitably ruins the punch line. Should I ask him to translate, or is that eavesdropping?" Silas had spent his youth enjoying Warner Brothers cartoons, so anthropomorphizing nature was instinctive.

"I'll bet he's fluent in monkey and its various sub-dialects," he considered. "He probably knows the reptilian slang for capybara, which is pronounced with a Castilian lisp, and some choice swear words in Toucanese that are incomprehensibly vulgar and shockingly racist, given the lovely complementarities of its close family members."

Airto pretended not to notice the growing attention he was receiving from Silas as he steered the boat from the main river body into a narrow tributary choked with trees and submerged logs. The sides of the boat rubbed against dense growth that endorsed the flanks of the craft with a series of notches before allowing it to continue on its way, resembling an old steamer trunk that had been checked and stamped through customs on the Grand Tour. As Airto pushed the tree limbs aside, he used them to propel the craft like a series of barge poles; with his other hand he tilted the outboard motor forward so that the propeller would clear the tree stumps that loomed beneath.

Pushing through the leaves and detritus, they finally emerged from the channel into a large open lake that shown like an opal beneath the midday sun. Their sudden appearance surprised a troop of howler monkeys who scurried along the shoreline and then flung themselves upward into the protection of an awaiting tree.

Silas listened intently to their mischievous chatter and tried to decipher its meaning. The agitated calls rang out across the lake, receiving sufficient recognition that the sounds were echoed from another location in close proximity, the direction of which Silas was unable to discern.

"Reflection, repetition, imitation." Silas allowed his inner thoughts to emerge. He wasn't speaking either to John or Airto specifically, but simply vocalizing his impressions to be heard or ignored, it didn't matter.

"You say this, I repeat it. I add an inflection, it bounces back, the inflection is absorbed into the pattern. A gradual change has occurred. A mutation. Did you hear it? A simple modulation of frequency. A concert A-natural became a B-flat. A change of attitude.

"Like Miles Davis and John Coltrane exchanging riffs. It's elemental, stacking layers of ideas like a step pyramid. A sotto voce subtly altered to a mezza voce. The sound permeating the warm air without revealing the hidden location of its vocalist. The conductor of nature, fine tuning its orchestra. The music of the forest. Its grief and agony resonant in shrieks, howls, groans, yelps.

"What would this earth have sounded like if it were a little bit smaller and the atmosphere less dense, and perhaps a different chemical formulation, say helium methane and potassium gas instead of nitrogen and oxygen? What odd eruptions and blasts of noise would have permeated the aether? Horned and fluted, bellowed, accordioned, and rattled or tambourined, what kind of instruments would have protruded from the lungs, gills, sinus passages, and seething orifices of the creatures that inhabited this world?"

John grinned at his new friend. "I was wondering when you might return to us." This was the Silas that he had first encountered back in the lobby of the Institute who casually held court with the group of new hires, rambling histrionically before the baffled newbies. "I'm glad you're feeling better," John said warmly, and then impulsively slapped him on the back. "I was afraid for a moment that I would be making this trip alone."

"Not a chance. It takes more than a little stomach flu to shut me up."

"I knew you had a keen interest in language, but I didn't realize I was traveling with Dr. Doolittle." The trumpeting of an Ocellated turkey from the nearby underbrush startled them. "Sometimes a noise is just a noise. Not everything is meaningful or supplies information."

"Too true." Silas complemented John on his observation. "Several years ago, I spent the day sifting through an excavation at the Calico Early Man Site. I was working next to an amateur anthropologist who decided that every rock he scraped out of the ground was a manmade tool or some kind of skilled artifice. It was clear to me that these were plain old igneous rocks, but he couldn't be dissuaded. The human mind wants to find patterns and associations that make sense out of randomness. Like the galloping unicorns that people witness in the fluffy clouds that drift across the sky, our perception wants to rationalize the irrational. We live in a Snickerdoodle world of sorts. The dough has been kneaded and spread over the cutting board, and our cookie-cutter minds press the little animals that we see."

"Oh, don't give up that fast," John said. "I was

enjoying your little monologue on...what was it, the meaning of animal farts?"

"I'm not calling a truce. I'm just acknowledging your comment as a courtesy."

"Don't get me wrong, Silas. I'm not saying that the animal noises are not purposeful, it's just that they are conveying information in a manner and for a reason that you may have overlooked in your desire to see them as sentient creatures. Let's take the example of a quartz clock oscillator aboard a satellite that's moving at about 7,000 miles per hour. Due to relativistic effects and lower gravity the speeding satellite clock is out of sync with its earthbound receiving station, which has navigational consequences for the satellite. We call this problem *satellite clock bias*. The satellite clocks are typically synchronized with reference to a ground station, however, in a distributed network of satellites, each node, or in this case the *individual*, maintains its sense of temporal order by sharing its concept of time with each of the other nodes in the network.

"The correct epoch or time scale is established by the time delay between the reference pulse of the master satellite, or in this case the alpha male, and the various members of the network. Have you noticed that it is always the largest male that delivers the primary pulse, which gets repeated throughout the clan? The sounds you are hearing from the hoard of monkeys are not descriptions of *how* and *why*, but *when*. Your gossiping gibbons are exchanging notions of time rather than the salacious details of a mating ritual gone horribly wrong, or the comic pratfall of an ocelot slipping on a banana peel."

Silas scratched his head incredulously. "Yes, but the social construction of *Time* as such is a modern innovation. The first public clocks, that only counted hours by the way, didn't appear in Europe until the early 13th century, and they were engineered to help people remember to say their prayers. Animals don't have to catch the city bus, or race to make their afternoon appointment for tea and scones with the vicar. There's no such requirement for that kind of chronological specificity."

"Au contraire, mon frére," John said combatively in the only tortured bit of French that he knew. "We live in a clockwork universe, and though we may not notice it, the sequence of daily natural events is finely tuned. Circadian clocks of animals and plant species are accurate to within just a few minutes. Sleep-wake cycles, feeding, mating, and migration are directed by insulin pathways with a kind of Prussian efficiency, which would make field marshal Rommel salute and say, Jawohl."

Silas winced at the allusion to the Desert Fox. "First, it's French, now German. I feel like there is a *spicy meatball* lurking in my immediate future."

John dismissed the gibe and continued his rant. "Nature is punching your timecard all day long. Time is a relentless and unforgiving taskmaster. Your presumed mammalian quibbling about the scarcity of hazel nuts, the latest fashion in meal worms, or the attractions of riverfront property versus a used pangolin burrow in the heights came much later and is quite incidental to the prime directive. Time is everything."

Then noticing how contentious he was beginning to sound; John lowered his voice and began speaking in a tone that was almost apologetic. "This is the main point, the sounds we hear are synchronizing nature. Everyone plays their role, but they must be on the same page. Our brains can fall out of sync with reality. In humans, we call this schizophrenia and fundamentally. It represents an interruption of the individual's ability to process temporal sequences. Schizophrenics have essentially fallen outside of the normal time scale, and the brain's efforts to realign with the standard temporal mode results in processing errors that cause hallucinations. They are drifting in and out of phase with time. They have lost the narrative in the sense that their perception of chronology is deformed. The mainspring in their internal clock has become uncoiled."

Silas still seemed unconvinced as he casually swatted a water bug from his shin and tossed the offending carcass overboard.

"Let me put it another way." John attempted to appeal to Silas's musical sensibility. "When a piano is in tune, its strings vibrate sympathetically with a tuning fork. The agreement between the piano wire and the metal prongs produces a harmonic resonance. Some refer to this process as *truing*."

Silas didn't like being patronized, and he particularly didn't like his own foibles being used against him, nevertheless he waited patiently for John to conclude his remarks.

"Did you realize that every one of your individual cells is emitting sound at a specific resonant frequency?"

The question sounded more like an accusation than a polite invitation to consider an unusual physiological phenomenon.

"If you're using an ultra-microphone placed into the interstitial tissue, you can actually hear the sound that is being generated. Your entire body is droning like a honeybee, but it's not audible to our ears. Imagine what happens when someone who is droning in the key of C major encounters someone vibrating in the key of G-sharp minor. The dissonance would feel uncomfortable, wouldn't it? Perhaps even inspire some sensation of fear or aggression? Now what if a key of C person meets a key of E person? Best friends for life."

Silas recalled his childhood days where his home backed to the Pacific Coast Highway. He would lie in his bed at night and listen to the hum of the car engines as they decelerated into the intersection, paused briefly at the crimson traffic light, and then accelerated on their way. After a while, he became proficient at identifying various automobiles by their telltale exhaust, the throaty puttering of a VW's horizontally opposed cast-iron cylinders, the impolite belching and gulping of a supercharged Camaro, or the deep guttural rattling of a Peterbilt engaging its Jake brake. Silas was amused to think of people going about their day in a self-propelled clamor, bellowing methane and carbon dioxide as they made their way to their daily errands.

John interrupted his reverie. "Perhaps it's too obvious an observation to say that music is often referred to as the universal language. But unless you're Italian, it's not really a language at all, is it?"

Silas groaned. "I knew that spicy meatball was coming."

"Maybe I deserved that." John chuckled. "Music is not a primitive form of communication. I believe it's a kind of navigational beacon or a sounding buoy that informs its user whether their actions are complementary to nature or retrograde. It calibrates the individual, keeping them properly aligned and true. The resonance frequencies form a wave distribution across the brain's alpha patterns that restore the natural time sequence. That's why music and dance are so critical to social gatherings. It reinforces the internal clock. The harmonic isoforms found in Bach's music are more than merely a pleasant escape from one's present circumstance. They restore the corruption of time."

Silas sat for a moment, pondering John's remarks, while John impatiently awaited Silas's verdict on his sonic theory of time regulation, but none were forthcoming. Then Silas made a rather frugal donation. "It's not a bad theory, you know. Even though you lost your rudder, your fuel tank was empty, and your undercarriage didn't retract completely, you walked away from a pretty rough landing."

"I guess that's about as near to a concession as I'm going to get today." John laughed.

"Don't think of it as a concession so much as a temporary reprieve for the condemned," Silas retorted, and then sarcastically added, "You've escaped the electric chair today, but you're on your last appeal. Enjoy the fresh air while you can."

CHAPTER 13 – EXODUS

When Banik was a mere child, barely able to fill an entire bucket of water from the family cistern, he was forced to run and hide in the sugarcane fields of his grandparent's plantation to escape capture by rival villagers. Boys of his age were malleable. They could be trained to perform difficult and dangerous work, and if they died from injury or exhaustion, they were also quite expendable.

Crouching in terror, he shut his eyes as tightly as he could, believing that if he could not see his pursuers, then he would be invisible to them as he cowered behind the tall stalks of cane. He now realized that, as an adult, he was guilty of the same childish folly. He had shut his eyes to the growing corruption, believing somehow that if he acknowledged its presence, it made it real. And yet, it had taken residence in the very rooms of his own home, and he found himself thrown into the street, seeking amnesty from the mob.

Banik was walking at a brisk pace away from the besieged temple, hoping that his momentum would ward off any street peddlers. He avoided looking at people's faces for fear of recognition, or that they would see the fear in his own face. "Can people see that I am afraid?" he wondered. Banik had never seen his own face, as it was strictly prohibited by the monastic order. Self-adoration was the greatest of sins. It was well understood that self-love is the root of all evil. Ironically, it was the poor people of the city who could easily pick Banik out of a crowd. He now feared that his low brow celebrity would be his undoing.

Even as he was fleeing for his life, he couldn't stop taking account of the people he passed on the street. "The small girl by the flower cart is without shoes," he thought. "I think we have a pair in our donation cabinet that might fit her." Then realizing the futility of his impulse, he shook his head and chastised himself aloud. "What a fool I have been."

He quickened his pace, trying not to notice the unhappy child and began writhing on all the little things done and undone. His careful preparations and incremental goals, spectacular failures and modest achievements were on display as he made his escape.

Had his life's work here made any impact at all? In his mind he kept a running inventory of blankets, packages of food, and medicines that he rationed with great care as he triaged those who were most in need. Small lifelines of hope cast into darkness, grasped by the wretched crew of a sinking ship. What was the grand sum of his contribution? The poor are still there. For every person he rescued from oblivion, it seemed that another fell into depravity and mischief.

As he moved through the crowded streets, he saw the city with fresh eyes, as he once did when his father hoisted him onto his broad shoulders and took him to the marketplace for the first time. Then, from a narrow corridor off the main thoroughfare, he heard his name.

"Banik!"

He stopped.

"Are you alright? I heard they captured the temple."

It was Chaben, his old friend. How fitting that they would meet on this day, his last in the city. Chaben had been one of the first children to make his acquaintance as a schoolboy, and now it would appear, he would be the only one to say his goodbyes.

"I'm holding up as well as could be expected," Banik said, "but if you don't mind, I need to keep moving while we speak."

"Of course, my friend." Chaben fell into step with Banik's hurried stride. "But tell me is it true what they are saying? Did the temple sentinels and the monks attack a group of supplicants for blaspheming the ritual?"

"Ah, I see now how the web has been spun. So, we are the aggressors, are we?" Banik suddenly realized that the riot was not the result of a lone provocateur shouting epithets and vitriol on the street corner, and that the participants were not mere rabble rousers. Trained partisans infiltrated the mob and gave its people the backbone they needed to commit their heresy. "Remarkable," he gasped under his breath as the full weight of the conspiracy hit home.

"Sometimes the only thing that stands between civilized human behavior and atrocity is permission," Banik said. "Not all of us are imbued with common sense. There are those of us who have had disappointment in life, and they are readily disposed to acts of vengeance. They only require the permission of a demagogue to fulfill their retribution."

"But why?" Chaben implored. "The monks help us to understand ourselves through our connection with our ancestors. Why would anyone take offense to that?"

"It is precisely for that reason that we have been attacked. There are men who speak about heroic and brave action, a break with the past, and abeyance of tradition. 'Burn the history books, and pull down the statues,' they say. There are no great men, they insist, only great lies."

Just then, the great clock tower heralded the hour with an ill-timed and pathetic thud, which was a mockery of its essential purpose. The carillon once resounded throughout the city, striking like a thunderclap as the wavefront propagated with a warm crescendo, gathering in a cresting wave that released its energy in every household. For that moment, the entire population was united and bound together as one entity while the sound reverberated in their very bones, penetrating unseen places, and then dissipating into the sky and the earth.

Palinode – "Keeper of Legends"

When the clock mechanism fell into disrepair, the civil engineers shook their heads in disappointment. The clock-smiths who had fashioned the escapement and cast the enormous clock bell had gone into retirement, and the foundry, where massive crucibles poured liquid fire of molten bronze and silver alloy into iron molds, had been dismantled. A search of the city was conducted, and runners were sent to the four corners, but no one of competence could be found. The generations of apprenticeship and patronage that formed a long succession of skilled metal-smiths had been broken, and no one knew how to reassemble the culture that made the clock. At last, the knowledge was lost.

"Where will you go?" Chaben asked. "Certainly, the mob will come to their senses. Peace will be restored." He had said it hopefully, although not believing his own words.

Banik stopped and faced his friend. "This was a warning. They could have killed us in our sleep, or worse. This bit of street theater was only a presage of things to come. Imagine, they stormed the temple in the full light of day without opposition and under the watchful eye of the city fathers. Now that's power."

Then reluctantly Banik turned away from one of the few friends he had. "Look...you shouldn't be seen with me. Go back to your home and act like nothing has happened. When the time is right, I will send someone for you. Put your private affairs in order and gather your valuables into a knapsack...and be prepared."

"But...prepared for what?" Chaben revealed his confusion, having believed the event at the temple was an aberration and not indicative of a larger plot.

"This is only the beginning of something, not the end. I should have seen it...no, I refused to see it. Drip by drip, the steady erosion was taking place all around me, but I believed it was isolated, or at least I hoped it could be quarantined or stanched by good works as a kind of moral tourniquet. But now it's fully upon us. Your world is about to change in ways you didn't think was possible. This is a revolution."

Chaben's mind was quickly assembling the forensic evidence of this unseen betrayal. There were the unfamiliar faces in public institutions, mysterious disappearances, a barrage of harsh new rules with regards to public social discourse that amounted to an extravagance of moral posturing, limits on speech and travel, strange alterations in the conventions of language that seemed like it was translated from a forgotten dialect, enforcement of new codes of conduct and manner of dress, and a growing cult of catastrophism that sowed fear among the young, but also encouraged a sense of nihilism and wanton abandon that manifested in acts of self-destruction.

Taken independently, either one of these events was not cause for alarm, but the totality amounted to a fundamental change in the culture.

"It's been happening under my very nose, and I

couldn't see it," Chaben said with a tone of surprise.

"None of us saw it." Banik extended his hand in appreciation. And with that, the old friends parted company, both melding into the anonymity of the crowd.

The broad thoroughfares of Toltec's masterwork had become sclerotic, enclosed, and choked with people. The stone pavers worn into saucers from the heavy foot traffic; the pristine reflecting pools fetid and black with stinking moss and algae. Crowded tenements weighed down from above, and the subtle attrition of storefront and row house, steadily encroached into the human passageways. The suffocating air itself became a dwindling and rarified commodity, as makeshift buildings maligned the skyline. The crush of people eventually tunneled underground and huddled in suffocating burrows and catacombs like rats and dung beetles.

The once great city of Toltec was merely a dream unremembered. The exquisite cut blocks of limestone, the masterworks of generations of skilled artisans, were cannibalized and pulverized into hydraulic concrete and extruded into wooden forms, making a gridiron matrix that housed its citizens like unhappy prisoners in a high security cellblock.

The old guard had removed themselves from the turbulence of civic life and found sanctuary behind walled enclaves. They entertained themselves with solitary amusements, meandering in serene landscapes abundant with manicured flowers and climbing vines, cared for by diminutive servants with pristine manners and immaculate white gloves who were chosen for their discretion and lack of natural curiosity. It was a farcical rendering of the city's former glory.

Banik's position in the temple afforded him an insight into the workings of the city and its people that was unusual. He could spend his days serving the poor without any stigma, and then be invited to dine in the grand halls of the great patrons for supper. He easily adapted his demeanor so as not to appear condescending in the presence of the downtrodden, and just as easily assumed the role of wise but submissive council among the elites, occasionally steering their intentions by subtle persuasion, but never directly challenging their pretension.

The transformation was as simple as removing his canvas tunic and donning the silken finery of his hosts. Although he was not one of them, his position was acknowledged as a token of esteem for his sacred order. His presence conferred a kind of respectability on the proceedings, although he wasn't sure why. Neither he nor his brethren shared anything in common with their benefactors.

He was part of a matched set. Seated between a soldier of the line and an actress, and directly opposite from a financier, he completed an obligatory social custom that demanded a representative from each estate, much like the silver tableware with its requisite toolkit of spoons, forks, crab crackers, and cheese knives.

At times, he felt that he was a river between two shores. Each group could peer across the water and see people standing on the other side. Yet, no one was willing to wade into the fast-moving current, lest they be swept away.

He privately harbored resentment for the poor people for whom he quietly labored. "Why don't they just stop making mistakes?" he would think to himself in frustration. Some long-forgotten trauma had fueled a lifetime of self-abuse, which they happily lavished in heaping portions upon the community. He resented them for their weakness, and simultaneously felt pity for their inability to see the world beyond their own selfish desires.

Likewise, he felt little empathy for the trivial concerns of the elites who complained endlessly about minor insults and perceived slights that amounted to an infinitesimal preoccupation with social status. The massive public building project that had become their collective identity was perpetually under construction and was supported by a makeshift scaffold of lies, demanding the meticulous attention of a cadre of retainers and gushing sycophants. Their worries seemed manufactured, their grievances a cry for attention, their philanthropy an artificial substitute for a place in their soul that was reserved for a conscience, but like an expensive balcony seat at an unpopular show, it was left conspicuously unattended.

Banik was surprised by the welling of emotions that rose to the surface from feelings long beaten into submission.

"Why all of a sudden now am I allowing myself to feel rage?" he thought. "Why didn't I step forward when the gauntlet was cast...when some righteous anger might have done some good?" Spontaneity had been the victim of caution. And what he had convinced himself was that sacrifice for the greater good was a shrinking complicity.

Instead, every line that was crossed, was greeted with retreat. Every incursion into sovereign territory was met with capitulation. The shock troops of chaos breached every holdout. No wall was high enough that it could not be scaled, no armor resilient enough that it could not be penetrated, and no bunker so deep that it could not be unearthed.

The nervous chatter he had dismissed as the idle prattle of the self-obsessed and deluded, had taken hold like an infection. It began as mild discomfort, with a fever of dissent that rapidly advanced to coarse language and an erosion of public decorum. As the disease process advanced to its acute phase the blisters of resentment became festering wounds of lewd behavior and vandalism. Once it was fully metastasized, the contagion erupted as brazen assaults and a gangrenous violence that left the social connective tissue in a rotting, putrid state of rebellion.

Palinode – "Keeper of Legends"

Then Banik had a moment of realization. "Those drums? Where did they come from?" Every time he witnessed a gathering of the partisans, they were immersed in a riot of thunderous drumming. It had become so commonplace that he learned to ignore them, but the cadence unconsciously regulated his breathing, it adjusted his stride, it made him speak faster and louder...the subdivision of time was altering the social patterns of the city. The repetition produced a false timescale. It was counterfeit time or manufactured time. It replaced the pulse of nature with an imposed audioscape intended to reorient the individual to a new reality.

"They have been reorganizing the time collective through the hypnosis of repetition," he finally recognized. The chanting in unison, the slogans recited in rhyme, were all intended to create a new time signature. The damaged clock tower was no accident. The gearing and escapement were designed to last a hundred years. This is how they had managed to derail the entire civilization. Like a runaway train, the people of Yarpay were diverted off the main narrative onto a new chronology, and the lies became a mantra, and then a creed, and the creed was developed into a doctrine, the doctrine became articles of faith, with true believers and heretics. "How fast it had all happened."

"History doesn't exist," they proclaimed. "Morality is oppression...words are violence...nothing is real."

The goal of the new philosophy was the elimination of shame. It was decided by wise and learned men at the schools and the elites in the fashionable salons that the cause of human suffering was not the inability of men to master their own selfish desires, but instead, it was the sense of shame or disgrace associated with one's misdeeds. Therefore, they concluded, shame must be amputated from all human endeavors like some cancerous appendage and eradicated from human consciousness. No one would be judged for their deeds, no matter how deviant or destructive.

Enforcers of the new regime were recruited from the lowest quarters. Moral untouchables who disqualified themselves from participation in society through their indecent actions, were eager to exact their revenge wherever and on whomever they could.

The marketplace celebrated and embraced the new philosophy. Without shame there was no limit on what could be sold, or what fees could be charged. The slave markets were inaugurated in the town square and the prostitution of children was allowed to trade in the full light of day.

The money lenders established themselves in the opium dens and brothels where long lines assembled after the morning's call to prayer. The gambling rooms extended their hold over the poor, accepting contracts of indentured servitude for a chance to make a precarious wager. Passersby watched the billboards in stupefaction as last week's market prices were wiped clear, and the listing of novel acts of human degradation were placed on the monetary exchange as accepted currency, written provisionally in black grease paint. The exploration of chaos and decadence was monetized, and the safe investment was debauchery. Bitter commodities of loathing were traded like loaves of bread and bushels of corn, feeding the insatiable and the unappeased.

The merchants applauded and congratulated themselves that they had the sophistication to remove a quaint but cherished notion that had restrained them from achieving their greatest desires. And having been liberated from their shame, the people looked deep within themselves, and they witnessed the abyss, and it echoed back to them with praise and adulation. "You are a god."

Separated from the wisdom and morality of the elders, the people were left to create their own sense of purpose and derive meaning from the values of the marketplace, which was a multi-headed hydra of greed, lust, and self-infatuation. The discovery of self that Yarpay had made eons ago, led to great discoveries and innovations, but the obsession with self was destroying everything the Yarpayans had built. They no longer relied upon the gentle mercy of the environment to sustain them with scraps and drippings from the feast of nature.

"Why should we be satisfied with nature's meager

offerings, which it doles out in such miserly portions?" they asked. They drank whole rivers and scraped away at the crust of the earth. The alchemists and herbalists salvaged what they could. But the lineage of a million years had been severed. The close relationship of the Yarpayans with the earth was ended.

Banik pushed his way to the city gate so that he could make his exit before the portcullis was lowered at curfew. There was a long line of people waiting to leave, and each one and their belongings were being scrutinized by the gendarme.

Smuggling contraband out of the city was not easy. Goods are brought into the city, but they are not permitted to leave, unless that thing is deemed to be of no value, in which case the object is stamped with the seal of null by a customs officer, and effectively becomes excommunicated from the interior of the city as worthless.

Items of value that are seized at the gate are repatriated, auctioned, or melted down into ingots to create something new. The practice was intended to enhance the wealth of the city but led to a system of clandestine escrow agencies that operated just beyond its boundaries, charging rent for holding cash and valuables for travelers. The city had become a kind of urban vortex that swallowed everything from the countryside.

Separated from their belongings, even migrants could not escape the gravitational pull of the city core where they found themselves stripped of dignity and reduced to their functional value. Unable to raise the funds for the expatriate fee that would release them from their bondage, they swarmed in ghettos of resentment.

The temple eunuch stepped nervously toward the outer gate. Attempting to remove even something as mundane as a salt cellar could be severely punished, and risking a bribe with the wrong official could be dangerous. He tried to appear nonchalant as the propagation vials containing the seedlings of the Keeper weighed uncomfortably under his clothes.

A large family of seven just ahead of him was quitting the city for good, joining the growing migration of people who sought refuge from its corruption in foreign lands. The official was making them unpack their carefully arranged bundles and took pleasure in exposing the personal possessions and undergarments of each family member for all to see. It was the last insult in a litany of insults the family would endure at the hands of the uniformed guards. The creeping indignity of inspections and public reprimands forced them to relinquish their belongings and join the exodus for the frontier. Frightened by the shouting of the customs officer, a baby sheltered in her mother's arms began to cry. This was the last descendant of Toltec. She would never know the creations of her great ancestor.

"You there," one of the guards barked. "Keep it

moving."

Banik was startled by the command. In his effort to appear uninterested, he had lost his place in line, and was now attracting the very attention he had wished to avoid.

"Fall in line," the young guard ordered, who was a man of diminutive height and modest intellectual gifts compensated by a generous endowment of bravado and sadism.

"Where are you going?" the guard demanded.

"So, the interrogation begins," Banik thought, who had conscientiously removed every symbol of his status, which might have previously smoothed his passage through the checkpoint.

Affecting an air of casual indifference, Banik replied, "I have some business behind the wall. I shall be returning in a day or so, but not more."

"Why have you waited until curfew to begin your journey?" the guard asked. "The light is beginning to wane. If you are travelling alone, you are wise to return home and start out again in the morning. There will be no moon tonight, and the bandits will make an easy meal of you."

Banik was not expecting this. Alarmed that he might not be allowed to leave, he searched for an excuse that would liberate him from the city. "I am indeed grateful for your concern, however, my errand is a timely one. My failure to arrive at my destination as planned would, I'm afraid, cause my friends to worry unnecessarily."

Banik was simultaneously impressed by the guard's apparent concern over his safety and upset that he couldn't improvise a better excuse for his evening departure than mere tardiness. He hadn't anticipated the rigor of his interrogator.

"Step aside please." The guard motioned for Banik to move out of line and stand in an alcove adjacent to the guard station.

"This is bad," Banik thought. "Very bad." It was one thing to trade quips with the young partisan, but quite another thing to endure the scrutiny of a trained professional. This was not part of his escape plan, and he had not prepared a cover story with sufficient detail to justify his sudden departure. As he sat weighing his options, each one in turn seemed to result in his arrest and some manner of physical harm.

Then, as if on cue, the high-pressure guy strolled into the alcove. He had just finished gnawing the last morsel of tissue from a fried iguana tail, which he casually threw on the ground. He chased the greasy iguana with a swig of honey mead and looked around absent-mindedly as if the room were deliberately concealing a thought that had escaped from the dungeon of his recent memory.

Banik studied the man intently. He wore a woven leather brigandine that was fastened with an arrangement of straps and buckles that made it look as though the device was meant to constrain the wild impulses of its wearer, rather than a means of protection from an attacker. An ornate knife holster was slung from his left shoulder. Banik realized that the intricacy of the holster sheathed a weapon that was not standard military issue. Such a blade would have been the reward for long years of service or a prize for a heroic deed. And unlike the other protectors of the gate who wore simple leather sandals, he displayed the green anaconda leather boots of a patrician.

"This guy used to be somebody, and now he's nobody," Banik thought. "He was important, and then he fell out of favor. Now he's stuck watching the gate with the plebs. It's a punishment."

Banik felt like his chances of success were diminishing by the moment, and he was gradually being consumed by an awful sense of dread. "This guy is either full of resentment at his loss of status and wants to inflict his revenge on others, or he desperately wants to win back his title and prestige by proving his competence at running the gate by catching defectors," he considered. "I'll be the whipping boy of his vengeance or the sacrificial lamb of his ambition."

The guard's demeanor appeared casual and unrehearsed, though his every movement and gesture were carefully measured and had been choreographed to illicit an overall feeling of unease.

Banik's heart began to beat furiously. "Intimidation is half the job," he thought. "It's the cultivated elevation of tension and the prolonged suspension of anxiety that makes one brittle, susceptible...breakable. How many questions would it take to find the essential untruth?"

Standing before the city gate, he was facing a metaphysical gateway that was no less imposing and no less real than the engineered mountain of granite that encircled the city. Before him stood a wall of logic, with truth and confinement on one side, lies and freedom on the other.

Banik had witnessed one of these sessions when he was called to stand-in as a neutral party on behalf of a thief. Even as a bystander, the intensity of the interrogator made him uncomfortable, but he never imagined he would be on the receiving end of such an exchange.

The interrogator dropped himself into a stool directly in front of Banik and propped his boot on the bench beside him. It was a power move, for sure, demonstrating his formal disregard for polite conventions. Then a spark of recognition transformed his sullen expression into one of curiosity.

"Don't I know you? Banik, isn't it?"

Banik's heart sank.

"Say, what happened up there? It sounds like you and your friends got a little out of control." He said that with a grin.

"You know what happened," Banik said grimly.

"No, I want to hear it from you. This doesn't have something to do with why you're leaving, does it?"

The interrogator loved his job and lingered sumptuously on every word. Unlike the typical vagabond or common miscreant who he was apt to harass and harangue, he finally had a real prize on his hands.

Frustrated by his little game, Banik asserted, "I think you know more than I do, so why don't you tell me why we have been forced out of the temple and made to flee for our lives?"

The interrogator somewhat appreciated Banik's candor, but he wasn't going to make it that easy for him. "Questions of 'why' pertain to an overarching strategy, and as a mere foot soldier I am not privy to such high-level discussion, as I am sure you must be aware."

His remark about being a "mere foot soldier," which he stated with exaggerated emphasis, confirmed Banik's suspicion that the interrogator had once been someone of prominence and was broken down to a lower rank, possibly for insubordination or perhaps moral indecency.

"My unique province is within the domain of *how*, otherwise known as tactics. Although my expertise is a subset of tactics called logistics." And then expanding on the subject he continued authoritatively as if he were lecturing at the war college. "I am told to take the hill, and I take the hill. I move my armies into place, I dig trenches and fortifications, I erect siege engines and catapults. I undermine their foundations and cut off their wells. I seize their granaries. I isolate the enemy within their own city, and then I stand back and allow the enemy to destroy themselves.

"The presence of my army causes a panic in the enemy camp, and the citizens do my work for me. They hoard their supplies and act like savages to their neighbors. They steal bread and water from their friends and turn family members away from their front doors. Eventually the people riot against their leaders and send traitors into my camp to negotiate terms of surrender. The moral breakdown of their society causes their destruction, and I have not fired a shot. Just ask me, of the dozens of military campaigns I have waged over the years, how many resulted in a pitched battle? Go ahead, take a guess."

Banik was uncertain of this strange diversion into military theory. The role of Yarpay's military operations was not a matter deemed suitable for public discourse, and its maneuvering along the frontier was generally kept secret, so Banik was genuinely surprised by his interrogator's question. "I'm not really sure...I mean, I know there have been many battles. But why are you asking me this?"

"I thought you wanted to know why they have chased you from the city. Isn't that your question?"

Growing tired of his forensic manipulation, Banik said, "Yes, I want to know."

"You are a humble servant of this city. The citizens here recognize you as an agent of compassion, and as such they see some hopeful aspect of themselves in you. If they destroy you, it will becalm the entire population. No one will think to step out of line. And to answer my own question, I've never fought a pitched battle in my entire career. We terrorized the populace and they simply collapsed. So why are you such a threat, Banik? Why is it at this very moment there is a brigade of soldiers coming here to take you?"

The interrogator's last comment caused Banik to jump to his feet in alarm.

"I'll tell you why. They want a definitive break with history. History is mocking them. It tells them they are fools, villains, and cowards at every turn. You are the embodiment of history, and you remind them of their folly.

"I suppose they'll make a spectacle of you. There will be a show trial perhaps and charges of sedition. They will say that you undermined the public good. And therefore, you must be destroyed...but not on my watch."

Banik looked at the interrogator with surprise as he rose to his feet and grabbed Banik by his tunic and thrust him out the door, while shouting to the other guards, "I'm taking this one to the pit. A little massage therapy will be good for his conversational skills." The guards chuckled morbidly at the interrogator's seemingly endless arsenal of torture euphemisms as they parted and allowed the two to make their escape.

Looking over his shoulder, the interrogator could

see a small contingent of soldiers arriving at the guard post to receive Banik as their prisoner. He encouraged Banik to move quickly as they raced up a treacherous spiral stone staircase within one of the city watch towers. With his lungs aching for breath, Banik emerged onto a platform perched high above the city wall where a small observational glider was balancing precipitously from a sling at the end of a massive trebuchet.

Banik stared helplessly at the device for a moment and then the interrogator helped Banik into the cockpit of the glider and threw the harness over his shoulders and locked it between his thighs, and pulled the belt tight.

"But what about you? They'll know it was you who made my escape."

The interrogator smiled and placed his hand on his ceremonial knife. "There's not much use for an old soldier like me these days. Besides, I'm going to have a little fun for once."

And with that, the interrogator released the launch anchor. Banik had no time to make the proper weight adjustment or trim corrections. The launch system dropped the colossal 40-ton counterweight into the catapult basement, and suddenly the full weight of the helmeted stone head created in the guise of its inventor, Chikaj, leaned defiantly on the 100-meter swing arm, tearing the glider from its moorings. With a deep groan, the glider was un-tethered high into the air where its wings unfolded as it soared into the atmosphere.

Banik piloted his craft skillfully and without regret, knowing he could never return. He rode the current upward chasing a pair of eagles higher and higher who were caught in the swirling monsoonal updraft. Banik could hear the recoil of a volley of steam powered missiles fired in his direction, but it was too late. He was far out of range and soaring brilliantly into the heavens as the sky unveiled a crimson sunset. Carving a graceful arc, Banik rolled the airship in the direction of a home that was distant and long forgotten. He set his course for the southern skies, never to be seen again.

CHAPTER 14 – TERRA FIRMA

Airto maneuvered the boat onto a small sandbar that projected into the deep-water lagoon like a miniature version of the Apennine Peninsula. He leapt from the boat and pulled the bow until the stern was no longer buoyant and was resting on dry sand.

"It's not very far from here," Airto reassured his passengers. "But we won't make our destination by nightfall, so we'll set up camp for the night, and start again early in the morning."

Airto gathered up some dry palm fronds and ignited the leaves with a chrome Zippo he kept in his front pocket. The lighter was tarnished to a marbled patina of clay and river rust. As the leaves smoldered and burned, he used the fronds to sweep a small clearing on the forest floor of its fire ants, spiders, and less desirable bed companions, before erecting the mosquito tent where they would spend the evening.

Silas was still writhing over his lost battle to John. Similar to Airto's camping preparations, Silas had scorched a swath of property in his head that was a comfortable residence for the monomania that consumed his quiet hours. Delusions of mediocrity had made him hypercompetitive, and John's goading had intensified his natural obsession.

A giant fruit bat hung overhead, adorably consuming a banana with the same relish that a child would eat a waffle cone of Rocky Road ice cream.

Then without provocation, Silas suddenly exclaimed, "Bats."

"Pardon me?" John looked about, confused, expecting to see a cauldron of bats with voracious intention descending on their encampment.

"Yes, of course, why didn't I think of it before?" Silas said, scolding himself. Then summarizing John's earlier thesis, Silas began litigating the charges. "You made the argument that animals are calibrating their internal clocks through sound," Silas said in an accusing fashion.

John, who by this time had entirely forgotten their previous conversation, began to retrace his mental footsteps. "Ah yes, I suppose I did make that assessment. So good of you to remember." He said it with a note of sarcasm and thought, "Oh boy, this guy can't let it go."

"Yes, bats. They don't care what time it is, so long as it's dinner time. They are spraying sonic energy everywhere to produce an image of the world in sound, which means that they don't live in the present. They live in the future."

"Oh, how so?"

"It's like this. Bats create their own time field. The

architecture of a brain that functions in terms of sound waves versus light waves must operate differently. The sonic energy that is being used is not passive. In echolocation, they produce their own navigational signals. They are deliberately pummeling the world with sound waves. The subtle delay occasioned by sound waves must influence how information is being anticipated."

Realizing that he was in for the long haul, John put down his sleeping bag and rested his hands on his hips while hooking his fingers through his belt loops in a display of abdication.

"Look at it this way. The transmission of light-based or photonic information is virtually instantaneous and covers an enormous bandwidth. In terms of the amount of data that must be processed and digested, you're not just getting the kitchen sink, you're getting the entire kitchen, the dining and living room, the whole shebang. This method of drinking from the fire hose, so to speak, has huge storage and disposal issues.

"Animals that receive their cues from the environment using photonic energy are sifting through a massive data dump, discarding what's static, and preserving what's important. They are like archivists of the recent past deciphering and translating the weighty tombs that each second of energy deposits into the library. Deciding which historical events should be preserved for the future in the primary codex, and which events get relegated to dehumidified cold storage is staggering in its complexity, and it's happening in this moment, and the next, and the next.

"Just think about that. Every day you absorb visual information that is equivalent to all the books and letters in the Library of Alexandria, and then when you go to sleep, most of that information is burned to the ground by the Julius Caesar of your sleeping unconsciousness.

"Our awareness may only be nanoseconds behind reality, but in terms of 'real' time it is a ponderous and lethargic slog by comparison. The point I am trying to make is that we live our lives retrospectively, like the Monday morning quarterback watching an old film reel of an NFL game. We live in the past, assembling our version of reality from an archive of information that may be recent in terms of biochemical operations, but is truly ancient from the perspective of the photon."

Airto was listening quietly but attentively to Silas's conjecture. He had laid a ground cloth over the burned area and was driving stakes into the ground at the corners of the mosquito tent. He was curious about the two men in his charge who seemed quite different from the adventurer's he typically led into the forest in their pursuit of gold or river monsters.

These two were seeking a different kind of treasure, and the discussion of time set him adrift on a sea of childhood memories that spanned the centuries.

"But what of sound?" Silas continued. "Bats do just fine flapping about in the molasses of a sonic environment, but with reference to the stationary background versus moving objects, they have to make much better predictions about the future. The information they receive about the environment is not instantaneous, so they must combine an image of the recent past with a variety of possible future trajectories or outcomes. How the heck do they do it?"

The question, of course, was rhetorical as Silas didn't wait for John to comment and simply forged ahead with his theory.

"I believe they live in an imagined future that is a kind of multiverse, and they see our world in the rearview mirror. They manufacture a future of multiple possibilities that gets gradually reduced as the implications of returning sound waves eliminate each potential scenario. They live on the leading edge of the wave front and cast a retrospective gaze at the world. There's no notion of synchrony or time stamping or unifying the tribe under the communal drum. Bats are time travelers. They have seen the future, or at least many different versions of the future, and they catch their prey nostalgically."

The sun was beginning to set, and after their long journey, John was feeling the limits of his endurance. Rather than offer a complaint about Silas's time-traveling bats, he extended an olive branch to his young compatriot. "I think you have made a forceful argument, my friend, and well taken indeed. As I rest tonight, I will consider your future-dwelling bats and their many worlds." And with that, John lowered his banner and gracefully retreated from the battlefield, but he was no less convinced of his own argument.

Silas appeared to be satisfied with John's acquiescence, and the two prepared for the evening's slumber in the shadows beyond Airto's campfire.

The fire unrolled thick coils of smoke that ascended into the sky like a length of gravity-defying rope from the basket of an Indian magician, carrying bits of ember and a dark soot from logs of damp mahogany. A life of 350 years was giving its donation of heat back to the universe as the chronology of its existence was peeled away, ring by ring and vindicated into heaven.

Airto's ancestors had worshipped the life-giving sun, and Silas's soliloquy on the time-altering effects of light was not unfamiliar to Airto, who had heard such things said by the Mayan temple priests at Tikal. He had learned to read the hieroglyphs inscribed on the temple monoliths, tracing their outline with his fingers, and knew their stories of creation and apocalypse. The memories of his youth were welcome visitors, and they arranged themselves in succession like a receiving party at a wedding, offering him both comfort and congratulations on the long life he had achieved. He reclined peacefully and basked in the warmth of one hundred thousand sunrises released by the great tree into the orange campfire and felt redeemed once again by the baptism of smoke.

CHAPTER 15 - THE WORLD IS FLAT

Airto didn't know why he had lived so long. He had many wives in succession: children, grandchildren, and great-grandchildren, and had outlived them all. Civilizations rose and fell, volcanoes erupted with extraordinary violence, scarring the landscape and becoming dormant, fantastic flightless birds ruled masterfully over their empire, and then went extinct, and still he persisted, watching, witnessing, experiencing the joy of renewal and the agony of lost friends and loved ones.

For a long time, he believed it was his duty to continue the traditions of his village, imparting centuries of knowledge as a bridge between the past and the future, projecting their immortal humanity, if not for the preservation of their unique spirit, then for an appreciation of their sacrifice and profound love for their children. But the grief of separation from his family and the oddly conspicuous nature of his unchanging condition brought him to the seclusion of the forest where he was less a thing of curiosity than a protector and sage advisor to travelers and adventurers alike. He studied the two men under his protection and pondered. "To give them knowledge is simultaneously a blessing and a curse. Is innocence so bad?"

Airto lived in a world of incomprehensible dimensions compared to John and Silas. The trajectory of their short lives fulfilled an arc that rapidly ascended from adolescence to adulthood, reaching a kind of plateau in middle-age, and then a gradual descent into senescence that spanned the useful life of one of Airto's well-oiled machetes. His experience had been absent of the longitudinal acceleration characterized as the stages of life. Aesthetically, he lived on a two-dimensional plane that spread out across the horizon in all directions, with occasional hills and valleys, and the monuments that one associates with challenges faced and responsibilities accepted, but there was no clear terminus to his journey that made him consider the narrative of his wanderings as a closed loop. His purpose was in the moment. No hierarchy of intention. No pretext. Every action or inaction was a spontaneous imagining, a tinkering and exploration of novel solutions to life's Gordian puzzle.

Not only had he lived well beyond his years, but he had penetrated and tunneled into a place of deep time that extended into the dawn of human civilization. He had seen the long duration of the forest and understood it as a pulsing vibrant thing, gnashing its teeth like a fearsome beast, and other times cowering into submission. He saw its destruction through lightning fire, its rebirth and maturity to old growth, the funeral pyre of conflagration at the end of its life and witnessed the rivers moving in their course over a vast range of estuaries like the wagging tail of a dog, and at other times convulsing and frothing at the mouth, as a poisoned beast, its blood thick with infection. He had endured alternating periods of deluge that seemed as though the world would at last be submerged, and every creature drowned in the rising water, followed by interminable years of drought that bleached the soil with the sun's wrath, delivering a blistered earth stinging with wounds of salt squeezed from every pore and crevice.

A child from the port city once told him that a late summer shower was certainly a harbinger of the coming apocalypse. His short life was so compressed that even the ill-timed downpour seemed a calamity out of all proportion with his limited circumstance. Similarly, Airto understood his traveling companions' vexation at the riddle of time. "They simply haven't lived long enough," he mused. "They view time as a knotted cord tied around the waist of the penitent marking his years of deprivation. They circumambulate the celestial orbit as a test of endurance, and for each passage around the sun, they are rewarded with a new knot that hangs from their belt.

"How curious that mariners developed the same technique to mark their travel across the ocean," he thought. "In a moving medium with no reference point and no boundaries, a log line was cast overboard and hauled behind the ship by a weighted buoy and, as the sequence of knots raced across the deck, they were counted to determine the speed of the craft. "Is this the significance of the knotted belt?" he asked himself. "A terrestrial inheritance from an ancient seafaring people. Perhaps as a reminder that we are adrift on an intergalactic sea without end, and the only dimension we can measure with any certainty is our acceleration through the emptiness."

Airto regarded the two men with a kind of fondness that one might bestow on a toddler. And like a good parent, he carefully considered what stories to share with them. Fairytales offered a stern warning wrapped in sweetness to make the bitter lesson digestible. "What can I say that would prepare them and not leave them discouraged?

"They see themselves as stationary, holding firm with feet planted obstinately in the sinking sand as the tide washes around them. Yet, they are inextricable from the continuum. Time is the thing itself; it is protagonist and antagonist all at once. How much should I reveal of myself?"

Turning the matter over in his mind, he allowed, "It is good that they have come here, to be with me in this place and at this time. They are removed from their familiar surroundings. It upends their confidence and challenges their assumptions about what is important. That is why they argue. They are seeing themselves through a different mirror, and they are attempting to reconcile the reflection with the memory of themselves.

That is why it's good to keep moving.

"A stationary life makes you inflexible. The tree that is rigid can be toppled by the storm, while the tree that moves with the wind bows gracefully and survives another day." Then reassuring himself, he asserted, "They will not be lost or swept away. They are rooted in rich soil. And that is good. I believe I can show them a path. If they can only trust me, I will help them," he finally resolved. "This journey prepares them for the message."

Then reminiscing on his own experience, he felt almost envious of the transformation they were about to undertake and retraced his own steps.

"The frontier is a beguiling place, and in the rapture of discovery you can lose your way...lose your mind, even. There are caverns of perception that beckon one to venture into the abyss and strange obsessions that will come to recognize you. Like a stray cat starved for a companion, the compulsion will follow affectionately at your heels and take residence in your home. It wants to be fed and so it must be fed. It is nourished and it grows."

Airto turned to his traveling companions to share his experience, but the weary travelers have drifted off to sleep. He carefully stoked the campfire, adding some leaves and a tincture of herbs from his canvass pouch. The smoke from the burning offering would settle gently over the camp, relieving the pain of their sore muscles and quieting their anxious thoughts, allowing them a deep restful sleep amid the cacophony of shrieking beasts that inhabited the night.

"It is well that they rest. Tomorrow is a new day and a new beginning."

CHAPTER 16 – A NEW BEGINNING

Temporarily stunned by the unexpectedly violent end to what was an otherwise graceful descent, Banik unhooked his harness and fell a short distance onto the sand, landing with a thud. He had aimed for a water landing, but as he glided below the treetops, he clipped the branch of a Sugar Apple tree with his wing, which sent him careening into the shoreline.

The moon shone high overhead, drenching the forest in a melancholy sea of lapis and sapphire. Handfuls of white pearls were scattered across the still water as payment for the moon's nocturnal passage. Here in the seclusion of the forest, on the borderlands of the southern frontier, Banik lay on his back, absorbing the starry sky and feeling as though he was the last man in the world.

"Yarpayans never ventured this far," he reflected. He knew they would not come looking for him and that his estrangement from that foreign land was akin to wandering on the dark side of the moon. The generations of myths had done their work. It had been a consummate labor of fear. Tales of wild beasts and even wilder, faithless men lurking beyond the hills had made the curious and those imbued with an adventurous spirit, unsettled and circumspect.

The creatures that were unseen had grown formidable in their imaginations. Without the trophies of a successful hunting party, dressed, butchered, and hung from the barbs of iron meat hooks in the marketplace or living specimens paraded on display in wire cages as fearful curiosities in the circus arena, the phantoms of legend grew out of proportion to their existence, stalking children in their nightmares and invading the waking thoughts of travelers and shepherds alike who found themselves on the periphery of civilization...alone, unsheltered, and exposed.

Tranquil herbivores who spent their days gorging themselves on the frothy entrails of passion fruit with their long slurping tongues were re-imagined as merciless assassins, poised for ambush in the forest canopy. And the truly sinister saber-tooth cats, whose ruthless talents were in no need of exaggeration were imputed with incomprehensible mystical powers that allowed them to hypnotize and beguile their victims, luring men deep into the forest with their fatal charms where they sadistically toy with their prey before devouring them alive.

As Banik gathered himself together, he considered his surroundings and the extraordinary events that led to his escape. Only twenty-four hours ago he was resting comfortably on his cot in the dormitory, considering plans for a new herbarium. Now he lay exposed to the elements, neither guest nor intruder, but simply another combatant hastily penciled onto the roster in a game of raw survival.

Despite his present circumstance, Banik was unconcerned by the gruesome legends of predation that haunted this place. For the first time in a long while, he felt at peace. The city, his former home, had been excised from his consciousness like a cancerous appendage. Free of the stifling air and the oppressive throng, he was able to breathe easy for once.

"Far better to fall victim to a ravenous beast that ends your life in a single devastating blow than the slow moral disintegration of the city, which not only takes your life, but your dignity, as well," he considered while attempting to connect a cluster of stars in the sky with invisible thread that formed the great Ocelot, the patron of his birth.

He pulled himself from the ground with the assistance of his aircraft's broken stabilizer and was delighted at the prospect of a new purpose. He had spent his life salvaging the wreckage of a ruined civilization. Now he would be the architect of a new vision for mankind. Like a delicate seed pod adrift on the breeze, he had found the fertile soil where he would take root. He was suddenly exhilarated at the chance to start anew. This was not the end of his story; it was merely the beginning.

The twisted and obstreperous vines that blanketed the dimly lit landscape no longer seemed a thing of menace and foreboding. The lush overgrowth welcomed him in a warm embrace like a battle-scarred soldier returning from a distant and prolonged campaign. This would be his home, a place of refuge and sanctuary for the righteous.

He reached within his tunic to make sure the delicate seedlings were secured. The tight cluster of silver ampoules were spared from the concussion of the plane crash as they had been carefully prepared at the temple in a bundle of cotton mesh infused with beeswax.

Luminescent eyes peered inquisitively from burrow and roost, ornamenting the night with blinking jewels of red, orange, and green as Banik adjusted his belt and unrolled his sleeves. He walked into the shallow water at the river's edge and enjoyed the turbulent flow around his feet and ankles. He cupped his hands, drawing cool water to his lips, tasting its sweetness, and then gulping thirstily. After drinking his fill, he splashed water on his face and neck and felt renewed. And yet, he felt a sudden pang of remorse for the future that was certain to arrive.

Just as the ancient astrologers imagined they could corral the stars into constellations with lassoes of gossamer, men would eventually bring this place to heel with surveyor's cord, level, and rod. This unrepentant and wild orphan of nature would be broken with illusions of meridians, base lines, and quadrants, and rationalized into utility as productive land for harvest and settlement. Plowed, terraced, mined, and drilled, it would hemorrhage its wealth of calories and minerals for an unyielding master.

"But it doesn't have to be that way," Banik insisted to the chorus of buzzing insects and croaking tree frogs. "This time we'll do it differently," he said aloud to the forest as though he were exhorting the mercies of an incredulous jury that was already convinced of the devilry of the accused.

"We will take as our example the honeybee over the hover fly. We will do our work, pollinating wild berries and melons, but this time leaving something sweet and delicious in return as payment to the earth."

Banik climbed the steep embankment from the shore, slipping and falling to his knees, he scraped at the sandy loam with his fingertips, exposing the dark red mineral rich earth beneath. He awkwardly clawed his way above the floodplain despite the sinking sand and turned to survey the land below. His life made sense now. He had been made to bear witness to the end of one civilization so that he could begin another.

In the distance, Banik could see the haunting blue glow of a thousand fireflies that sparkled like the tail of a comet that rained to earth and bounced and ricocheted in the tall grass. He was drawn hypnotically by the opulent display of insect eroticism, his feet moving independent of his conscious awareness. Yet, as he neared the courtship spectacle, the population of fireflies retreated en masse, keeping just out of his reach. His pace quickened as he pursued the winged creatures deeper into the forest, chasing their contrail through a wooded glen where a dense fog had settled for a night's rest and was suddenly illuminated with a diffused organic light as if it were a prelude to a waking dream.

He watched in amazement as the glowing swarm floated toward an outcrop of ancient granite that was buttressed and arched by eons of punishing heat and freezing cold, that had worn small cracks into the stone, until the cracks became fissures, and the fissures spread throughout the mass of stone, causing sudden rifts and areas of cleavage, leaving a fractured monument to the vicissitudes of time.

The luminous body of insects poured itself into the edifice as though it were from a jug of honey, until the night air once again grew dim, and the hollow interior of the rock pile was filled with a ghostly aura that sent a beam of light heavenward through a broken crevasse, where tons of rock had once fallen from the inner vault and crashed to the floor of the chamber. Over time, the interior of the formation had filled with soil that grew thick with dense mats of algae, and the chimney that was revealed by the collapse of rock from the ceiling admitted just enough light and rain to provide shelter for the delicate hanging primrose that carpeted the floor and adorned the walls of the cave with a rich lavender.

Banik dared to venture into the cave. Whether it was the courage inspired by his awakened passion, his innocence of the perils of his desperate condition, or his enchantment with the wondrous fantasy the pageant of nature had arranged for his pleasure, he was blissfully unaware of his circumstance as he emerged from the shadow of night into the suffuse radiance of the inner chamber. Standing in the center of the granite vault, whose walls were pregnant, glistening with bits of garnet and azurite, he was surrounded by a maelstrom of fireflies that descended on the cave primrose to devour its sweet nectar.

At his feet, amidst a sea of lavender, was an eruption of a fierce scarlet Crown of thorns digesting the last rays of moonlight. Banik reached into his tunic and retrieved the carefully wrapped ampoules. He dug a small hole in the damp acidic earth and removed one of the seedlings from its vessel. He carefully placed the roots into the ground and then after rolling up his sleeve, liberated a sharp thorn from one of the scarlet flowers. He pressed the thorn deep into his flesh until the blood bubbled forth in great profusion. He drenched the young seedlings with his blood to restore and fertilize the plants as the acolytes had always done. The Keeper was a chimera of human and plant, and the donation of blood was essential to its growth and survival.

"May you thrive and bring forth new life, while your roots grow deep and help us to remember ourselves, our living past," Banik uttered. And so began his vigil.

CHAPTER 17 - DREAM TIME

John awoke peacefully from a deep slumber that was ornamented with vivid dreams of a celebration that had assembled old friends, both living and dead. There was no purpose or pretense for the celebration, and it seemed to have lasted for days or even weeks on end. The guests shared stories with one another, and the sound of laughter rose and fell like waves cresting and releasing their energy in an explosion of white foam, only to retreat under cover of a wash of bubbles to reload and crash again.

"How odd that I've never noticed this color before," he observed. The proceedings were enshrouded in a warm light that did not appear to be localized on an exterior source, but instead seemed to emanate from within the revelers themselves as though joy itself had initiated a unique spectral response that was calibrated to the mood and enjoyment of each participant.

"At the periphery of our atmosphere where thin air is first touched by the light of dawn, there must be some increment of luminesce space where this color is rationed in discrete amounts in the realm between darkness and the aurora borealis," he imagined in his dream. "Surely, it's the most beautiful color of all."

Palinode – "Keeper of Legends"

For once, he was well rested, and the delirium of sleep that typically hovered like the morning fog had evaporated at first light. Airto had generously prepared a pot of rice porridge and an extravagant portion of smoked pork belly, which was simmering on the campfire. The aroma of cinnamon and almond mingling with the wild boar was a happy inducement to fold his knapsack and begin the day. John looked over at Silas who was still sleeping soundly and decided to let him enjoy another twenty minutes before playing reveille on the side of his mess kit.

Silas had been dreaming about his future-dwelling bats and realized the connection between the satisfying resolution of a harmonic chord and future time. "It's not just bats that are living in a future construct," he realized. "Melodies in some way are a probing investigation of future time," he mused. "The final chord is out there somewhere in your imagination, and the melody meanders and wanders this way and that, exploring different modal domains, sometimes lingering on a preening falsetto, and other times racing across the fields of a breathless arpeggiated soundscape, or thundering underneath the floorboards with a reedy vibrato. The independent streams of sound always return to the main body of sound, the root chord is the river, and all the tributaries must dissolve into the river that flows out into the sea of time."

In his dreams, which seemed strange and wonderful, he had enjoyed listening to the opening strains of an unfinished symphony that was voiced with the ethereal resonance of a hidden orchestra, concealed somewhere offstage. The familiar twelve-tone scale his ears had grown accustomed to hearing expanded by halves, then thirds, and fifths, and continued broadening and growing wider until each note revealed its own internal register.

The logic of a new harmonic underlying the substructure that he once believed was settled business, was exposed with each note revealing itself as a complex potion compounded of ingredients that were bitter and sweet, like tart cherries, wild honey, and aromatic cloves.

"And why shouldn't it be this way?" he asked himself. "The essential quality of any given thing is the summation of the constituents of its creation."

"'Ontogeny recapitulates phylogeny,' isn't that what they always say?" The embryo reproducing the entire history of its evolutionary past, from gilled fishy creature to burrowing mammal.

"Perhaps there is an entire symphony encapsulated in a single resonant frequency, and the entire history of the invention of the universe is being recapitulated in every sonorous tone. Maybe that's why music is so compelling. It's a return to first principles. As far out and dissonant as music becomes, there is an awareness that there is a root chord at the center of it all.

"Kepler's harmonics derived from the orbital ratios of the planets, and he proposed that the planets were singing their way through the universe as members of a grand celestial chorus. Can we hear it? That subtle music of the solar system must pervade everything and everyone.

"The hollow bells of the asteroid belt, and the shimmering strings of Saturn accompany the mournful bellowing of Jupiter's roaring skies, and the thunderous eruption of a Venusian volcano. Then suddenly, a lonesome soloist, an icy comet takes the stage, singing sweetly, abandoned, and forlorn as it searches the cosmos beyond the simmering lava worlds and massive gas giants."

Suspended in this lyrical state of wonder, a thin beam of light touched Silas's eyelids, candling his dream world in an embryonic yolk of orange and yellow as his concealed pupils constrict in anticipation of the waking moment.

Silas clambered along the swinging rope bridge of consciousness from the haunted island of sleep, ascending the jagged and splintered planks to the treacherous island of wakefulness, arriving on solid footing just in time for the tenuous rigging to unravel and collapse into the shadowland that lay between the two worlds. Yet, another narrow escape from the yawning abyss. How many times had he made the journey, stepping onto the visceral plane as the bridge fell asunder? How many crossings would he be permitted before he too fell into the void? The question had been troubling him with greater frequency than usual, and he wondered if the subconscious reminder was either a call to arms or a petition to surrender to a deeper sleep than he had ever known.

Silas was suddenly aware that he was being observed and opened his eyes to see John and Airto staring at him curiously.

"Well, that must have been some dream."

Silas was confused and even felt a little betrayed that his dream state might have had an audience.

"You've been humming and singing so pleasantly in your sleep that I didn't have the heart to wake you." John responded to Silas's obvious bewilderment. John handed him a bowl of rice porridge, and he propped himself up on one elbow and began eating. The echoes of his dream were fast departing. Airto's breakfast tasted good, and the pleasant mélange of sweet spice and savory flavors on his palate made his surroundings seem less strange and more familiar.

"Airto says that our objective is not far off," John said. "He seems certain that this plant we are seeking and his 'Keeper of Legends' are one and the same."

Silas nodded approvingly while he finished the last scoop of his porridge. "Yes, but has he explained why he believes our cryptid and his, what did he call it...*Keeper of Legends* are the same animal?"

"While you were sleeping, I pressed him for more details. He said that the plant has human memories, ancient ones, and that it speaks to those who are prepared."

"Prepared? Prepared for what? That sounds slightly ominous. Look...I don't plan to spend the next forty years out here in this wilderness, but if he can get this bush to speak, I'll follow him to Midian or Mount Sinai, or anywhere else he wants to go."

John chuckled at Silas's unregulated apostacy. "For the record, if this thing makes you the vessel of its wisdom, then it's *golden calf, here I come.*"

"You needn't worry about me," Silas replied. "I am a cruel but just leader. Your suffering will be exquisite, but brief."

Airto, who had been quietly listening to the two men as he dowsed the fire and folded the mosquito tent, wasn't sure what to make of his companions' verbal jousting. At times they seemed almost brotherly in their mutual affection, and then without warning they would begin this spontaneous verbal wrestling like a couple of mischievous lion cubs, tumbling with sarcasm.

Keenly aware of the hastening sun as it stretched its shoulders and grimaced before lifting the earth high above its head, Airto said, "I think we should begin our journey while the day is innocent." He pretended that his sense of urgency had to do with some hidden timetable that made the forest run like a Bavarian rail station, yet his true intention was to avert another lengthy digression from amassing its share of folly.

The men nodded in agreement, and with a renewed fervor, the three companions broke camp and set off into the forest.

CHAPTER 18 - UNMASKED

Airto moved with the grace of a young athlete as he negotiated an easy path for his traveling companions. Against the dense backdrop of the forest, which appeared impenetrable at times, he always managed to see an opening, or a path of least resistance where they could press themselves through the knotted and tangled biomass. Sometimes, when it appeared they had met their match, and might have to retrace their steps, Airto would suddenly push aside a branch, revealing a trace where just before, none had existed.

John and Silas would look at each other in astonishment, shaking their heads in disbelief as the sturdy forest guide continued to forge ahead without breaking stride.

As John observed Airto, he realized he was witnessing someone whose expenditure of energy was perfectly balanced with his conservation of movement. From his hands to his feet, his entire body was working in perfect unison to exert a determined forward effort that seemed so natural one might have guessed that he was propelled by some mechanical force like the moving pedestrian walkway that had carried them from the airplane terminal to the baggage carousel in the Aeropuerto Internacional Benito Juarez.

Airto had warned them to be alert for the deadly Fer-de-lance and the no less insidious Jumping Pit Viper, but at the rapid pace they were tracking through the lowlands, there seemed little chance of them gaining the upper hand in such an encounter.

Suddenly, Airto stopped and motioned to John and Silas to keep quiet. The two men dutifully held their breath and remained still. John could hear his heart beating in his eardrums and wondered if the rapid thumping was audible to his friends. Silas flashed a worried expression toward John, which he interpreted simultaneously as both "What is it?" or "I think I have to pee." Given the circumstances, he opted with his first instinct and shook his head as if to say, "I don't know." Then in the distance they could hear some voices that were moving in their direction. Airto turned. "Stay down, and don't move."

Through a small clearing, John and Silas could see a group of five men walking toward their position. Three of the men were carrying a young jaguar in a bamboo cage, which they supported with a triad of poles that rested uncomfortably on their thin shoulders. The remaining two men, one in front and one behind, were armed with rifles. The men holding the jaguar cage were arguing that it was time to trade places, and that they had carried the beast long enough.

Then, to John and Silas's utter surprise and

dismay, Airto emerged from the forest to stand directly in front of the procession.

Silas turned and whispered to John, "Is he crazy?"

John raised his hand to quiet Silas while thinking, "If they murder Airto, how are we going to find our way out of here?"

John and Silas continued watching the events unfold from their hiding place.

Airto walked casually over to the cage as though unconcerned by the presence of the would-be poachers and forced his fingers between the bamboo poles that had been conscripted for the makeshift travel crate. He tickled the flank of the young jaguar, and the act of affection was returned by the cat, appreciatively rubbing its muzzle and ears against his hand.

While continuing to stroke the cub's fur, Airto addressed the men without looking at them. "Why have you taken my cat?"

Despite their greater number and weapons, the men reacted with alarm to his query, which seemed out of all proportion to the imbalance of the circumstance. One of the men clumsily offered a kind of apology, stammering, "We-we didn't know it was your cat. If we had, we certainly would not have removed the animal. Please forgive us our indiscretion."

Airto turned toward the man who had spoken on behalf of the poachers, and in as matter of fact a tone as one might order a piece of toast and cup of coffee he said, "This cat, and every cat belong to me. Everything that crawls, every plant that blooms, every tree that bears fruit are my ward, from the hills to the valleys, and the headlands to the rivers that flow out to the sea."

Then turning to the other men, Airto spoke to them in an Olmec dialect that John and Silas had not previously heard. His voice was soft and constrained. It was neither chiding nor berating, but rather had a quality of sadness. The poachers were visibly shaken by the encounter, and even appeared aggrieved by their actions, offering Airto their weapons.

John and Silas observed the spectacle in awed astonishment. Continuing to speak in the low somber tone of a man delivering a eulogy, Airto gestured toward the sky, and then grasped the fruit of a morro tree. He easily broke the nearly impenetrable shell of the hard fruit in his hands and proceeded to spread the contents over the brow of each one of the poachers, who expressed relief at his intercession on their behalf. The men promised to make amends for their actions and returned in the direction of the river.

Airto then released the jaguar cub from its captivity. The cat briefly hesitated at the threshold of its enclosure, and then as if it had suddenly remembered an urgent appointment, it bolted into the forest and disappeared into the undergrowth. Airto returned to collect John and Silas from their hiding place, and upon seeing their stunned expressions he tried to offer some explanation for what they had just witnessed.

"Many men would claim that they have no choice.

That it was temptation and poor circumstance that made them do wrong. They would blame their mothers or brothers, or an unhappy childhood, or some unfortunate event that made them turn sour. But these men know me, and I know them. There are no accidents. Every moment is carefully constructed in our minds as if designed by the most scrupulous engineer. They willingly partake in this offense as a deliberate corruption of truth. It is a fascination with evil that beguiles them. They know this. I know this, and now you know this."

John and Silas were taken aback by his directness. They had been carefully groomed in a society that coddled criminals and rewarded corruption as the appropriate balance to something vaguely brandished as economic inequality by the grifters and hucksters in the political sphere. They had been told that all villains were merely victims of a patriarchal system of oppression. They knew better, of course, but no one had told them otherwise. Until now. Airto paused to allow his words to marinade in the salty brine of their cerebrospinal fluid. Then pointing at a troop of Howler monkeys who had been watching them with detached interest from the safety of a tall Ficus tree, Airto explained why he despised monkeys.

"They were once like people, animated with a divine spirit, with the understanding of good and evil, but they were given to hedonistic and decadent ways, reverting to a primeval state. The creatures you see before you are not the innocent children of the forest. They are the inheritors of the damned and the wretched. They gave up their humanity for pleasure, and their beastlike obsessions have become manifest."

John caught Silas drilling into his forehead with an expression of intensity and understood immediately because they shared the same thought. "Who the hell is this guy who is leading them into the forest?"

And they both suddenly realized that they weren't necessarily running the show as they had once believed. Their guide was no ordinary scout who one might bribe with a case of Pilsner and a carton of Marlboro Lights to divulge the secrets of the giant catfish lair. He was someone of eminence. Even a band of lawless poachers wouldn't dare cross the strange man of the forest, fleeing from his sight like scared children.

He had his own agenda and far from fulfilling their plans, they were enacting his design. He was directing them toward a purpose. But what could it possibly be? How did they find him anyway? Who recommended him? Was it the bush pilot? Neither John nor Silas could seem to remember how they were joined to their escort, but the decision was made for them, and for better or worse they would have to see it through to the end.

CHAPTER 19 –GARDEN OF DELIGHTS

Banik's donation had taken root and was fruitful. His devotion saw the propagation of a new colony that flourished and grew in wealth and complexity in its isolation, just as it had shunned the disparate and cacophonous voices of the outside world, whose barbarity had devolved into a narrow fascination with all things excreted and secreted.

The spark of insight engulfed Banik's adoptive children in only a matter of generations, spreading like a conflagration, and as it did so, the burning cinders of human imagination became weightless and were carried on high in the fast-moving trade winds, causing the fire to expand rapidly and ignite new spot fires that raged in all directions. And then when it was time, his descendants elected to cast aside the gentle reassurance of their earthly nursery and seek out the mature austerity of adulthood in the vacuum of the interstellar void, abandoning their birthplace to allow another species to emerge and achieve ascendance in their own right.

Born from the demise of the corrupted Yarpayan civilization, Banik's people shed the bonds of earth and became creatures of twilight, moving into the universe without regret. But how long had it been since the inheritors of Banik's city un-tethered itself from the world and drifted into the skies?

***

Airto often considered the strange fate of his ancient ancestors as he carefully winnowed a safe but narrow passage through the crooked terrain, briefly stopping to acknowledge the majesty of his surroundings. Would they return for him? He had walked this land for centuries, dutifully preserving their memory while looking for a sign, some implication of a reunion.

As he overlooked the welcoming arms of a lush valley populated with the broad canopies of old growth forest and punctuated with the precocious emergence of a new and fragrant verdure, he invited his two companions to step forward and enjoy the grandeur of the resplendent panorama.

John and Silas edged closer to the precipice, while Airto rested his hand on a jagged rock face, running the tips of his fingers along its horizontal ridges that comprised a layer of deposition that in the width of his palm encompassed more than 5,000 years of human history.

"Everything turns to stone," Airto thought. "Our bodies ossify and become rigid. Our notions become torpid and unyielding. Memories become fixations, reminiscence, chiseled and engraved totems frozen in blocks of wood and stone. Do rocks have memories?" he wondered.

From on top of the rugged outcrop, Airto could see how the four-dimensional space of human history was compressed into two dimensional planes and arranged as limestone sheets, folding entire civilizations into a neat envelope of stone, and arranged in sequence like a pile of old newspapers, their urgent headlines long since faded into oblivion.

Love, hope, longing, grief, tragedy, obsession, a slow and tortuous accretion of spent energy, exerted in the cause of survival, layered into a thin crust of aggregate. A thin grey line of humanity, ground under the imprimatur of geological forces, like the ruler of time pressing his seal into the permanent record of man to be stored away in the volcanic archive of the deep earth. In time, the heavy layers descended into the fires of Hephaestus where the human cement was annealed into a fine polished glass. Rich veins of lime-green marble and flecks of gold intermingled with pulverized tooth and bone. Linear bands of mortar in a mosaic of time.

"If human history is the product of geography, then geology is certainly the end point of biology." Airto carelessly threw a pebble into the valley below. He had grown weary, and for once was beginning to feel his great age. It was a sensation he had never experienced. "Is it finally my time?" he wondered. The notion of having completed his journey excited an array of feelings that vacillated between contentment and gratitude, then resignation and sorrow.

He felt the magic that made him a denizen of this forest and a strange outsider to all men finally relinquish its hold. He paused to consider its significance. "Is there any difference between a deep slumber and non-existence? Does the universe keep an inventory of retired souls as they are removed from the world of experience and vanish into nothing? I should think not," he resolved with some sadness. "Perhaps if I were to live in someone else's dream, inhabit their thoughts for just a moment, I could live in the gloaming, and as they rose from their sleep, they would remember that I was once a part of this world."

Having supped their fill of the forest pageant, John and Silas had been cautiously observing Airto for several moments, who seemed absorbed in some distant memory. "Had Airto lost his way?" They wondered about their solemn friend as he gazed far, far away, above the tree line and the steep hills beyond.

John and Silas looked at each other nervously. Airto was their lifeline and primary exit strategy from this place.

Then Airto broke free of his reverie and acknowledged his companions with a smile, letting them know that he was present once again, and reassured his guests. "It's not far from here."

Their reward close at hand, John and Silas moved with a renewed vigor. The anticipation of their journey's end relieved their aching muscles and seemed to propel them forward as though the wind, and even gravity itself, was in their favor. Soon, patterns began to emerge from the twisted land. Gentle undulating slopes became terraces and embankments. Rivulets of meandering streams found themselves requisitioned into narrow channels. And an outcrop of exposed bedrock showed evidence of tool marks where masons had once split longitudinal sections of brilliant white marble into slabs of building material. The all too familiar feeling of human intervention on a massive scale was making itself known by the fractal contours of nature giving way to the Euclidean shapes implicit in human-made forms that have been lovingly cast, tortuously hammered, and exquisitely sculpted and bronzed.

John and Silas began to perceive squares and rectangles on the ground, as well as right-angled walls, the telltale signs of nature doing man's bidding. As an ornately striped neckband snake hurried past his feet, Silas suddenly realized the elegant simplicity of the right-angle. More than any other feature, it is the right angle that defines the peculiar living quarters of humans. It was an invention so propitious and widespread it has entirely lost its significance in the course of time.

"Motion is danger." Silas continued his thought without waiting for an invitation to elaborate. "The mechanism of man's binocular visual system compares motion sequences in the foreground to the stationary objects in the depth of field. Predators with their sneaky spots and trickster stripes learned to evade the visual systems of their prey, by interrupting their visual continuity, but man imposed a network of right angles on his environment to spotlight his adversary by measuring their size and speed between intersecting perpendicular lines. Time has erased the shock of this innovation, and the radical became commonplace, and then invisible."

John said, "You're saying that when we speak of 'enemy lines' we are literally talking about lines, like those on a sheet of graph paper?"

"Well, yes, I suppose so. Angled wall joinery was not only an efficient method of building a shelter. It allowed people to see. It's such a constant and so pervasive throughout human civilizations that it has become facile. Yet, in terms of a defensive feature, it's as revolutionary as the wall battlements, arrow slits, portcullis, and drawbridge of the medieval castle. Only later in human evolution would people embrace organic architecture, when the environment had become absent of large predators.

"The emergence of angles and lines beneath our feet is comforting, not because it implies an artificial boundary or separation from nature, but because it enhances our vision and extends our grasp." Silas was pleased with his summation of the use of right angles in ancient architecture and was expecting a critique from

John.

"I'll say one thing," John replied. "You've saved us the indignity of singing about the sequential elimination of beer bottles from a presumptive wall shelf on our little journey."

Silas was quietly annoyed by John's remark. He didn't like his spontaneous insights, which he shared in the lofty spirit of new discovery, being compared to a deliberate time-wasting activity of counting backwards.

"Is that what he thinks of me?" Silas asked himself. "A dilettante madly spinning his wheels?" However, Silas's temper had a shallow reservoir, and before long, the perceived insult was forgotten, and he was again ruminating on the significance of ancient building techniques.

From the appearance of their surroundings, the ruin was recently inhabited by someone who had fought back the invading forest with such courage that it seemed they might almost prevail against their irresistible foe. Special care had been taken in repairing and preserving the arched threshold that led to the interior space. A broken monolith, scarred with time, was repointed with lime mortar that had not yet cured in the humid air. The broad uneven steps that descended into a reflecting pool had been recently cleared of debris, and a layer of fungus was abraded with pumice, revealing a weather-worn marble veneer. Creeping vines, the alley cats of the plant world, were properly scolded and sent on their way. "But who was the caretaker?" John had been wondering, and his curiosity was soon rewarded with an answer.

John realized that they were entering the lair of the forest king. This was the domain of Airto. Far from the shimmering lights and belching engines of civilization, this was Airto's home and his sanctuary.

Seeming to intercept the thoughts of his companions, Airto said, "I first came to this place long ago, but even then, it had been abandoned for millennia." He guided his guests into what appeared to be a kind of arboretum. "Even the ghosts retired from their watch after centuries of hiding. If no one returns, a lonely vigil is nothing more than isolation, and the artifacts of a dead culture are but the phantom pains of an amputee.

"Try as I might, this lost city longs for oblivion. I replace the fallen rocks and scrape away the overburden. I burn the plants into retreat for a while, and salvage what I can. I am a caretaker of disintegration, the devoted steward of rot and ruin. And in the quiet hours before the dawn, when doubt rules like a tyrant wielding uncertainty in its war upon the most serene conscience, I think to myself, 'Am I the dreamer, or the one who is dreamed? Perhaps it would have been better if I were nothing at all.'

"But I haven't brought you here to see my collection of rocks. You're here for a purpose. I didn't know it before, but I know it now. It's surprising how the universe works. We think we are charting our own course, carefully scripting our narrative according to our design. Then one day you realize the trail you blazed, in an act of youthful defiance, simply uncovered a much older road that was there for centuries...a road that was engineered with such care that the crushed rocks and stone slabs that penetrate the earth to a depth of several meters, have gone unnoticed and become invisible, yet it is the immovable earthen bed upon which we venture. Blessed gifts from our ancestors. What corridors and viaducts must exist in the sky? Tunnels and broad thoroughfares of cosmic dimension that bridge the interstellar trade routes of galactic civilizations. Grand armadas of a thousand ships or more must have departed from this base, thundering across the heavens to encounter some distant shore where they were received by a whirling pageant of ecstatic indigenes eager to receive their exotic wares, and share the sweet fruit of our world, while exchanging honored myths worthy of legend."

John and Silas looked at each other uncomfortably. They had journeyed a great distance, and at great personal and professional risk, in the hope of retrieving a plant specimen that would unlock the code to an anomaly they discovered in the human genome. Now they were faced with the possibility that their guide was not entirely sane, and that his claim to know the whereabouts of the mysterious plant species was just part of a delusion.

Airto invited John and Silas to make themselves at

home in what appeared to be a kind of cocoon. A lattice of branches that fanned out into a concave enclosure was coiled into braids as though woven together by an enormous pair of hands playing a child's game of cat's cradle. The limbs were coated in a fine velvet moss reminiscent of an elk's summer antlers. This is the one area where Airto had permitted nature to intervene of its own accord and take up residence in the stone compartments of the arboretum.

Airto lit a small stove with a match and coaxed the embers to life with dry kindling and some pungent herbs, their scent John and Silas remembered from the previous evening's campfire. He filled a tin coffee pot with water that was collected in a clay jar as runoff from the broad leaves of a banana tree, which procured sweet drops of dew from the lingering morning fog as it condensed and filtered into the thirsty soil.

"If you could speak to someone from a different world, what would you say to them?" Airto said abruptly, as he placed a small bundle of herbs into a mortar and began grinding the herbs into a fine powder with the tip of a well-worn pestle. Then continuing to prod at his guests he asked, "If you had only one thing to commute to the future, what would it be, a warning, an axiom, a syllogism, a code of morality perhaps?"

Neither John nor Silas was certain if Airto was speaking rhetorically, but not being one to shy away from a challenge Silas said, "Geometry...it's the connection between analysis and practice and is the basis of abstract logic. If you know the rudiments of geometry you can reconstruct civilization from its roots."

"But why would you assume the apocalypse?" Airto already knew the answer to his own question. "Why would you presume that the future is so delicate a place that it would have to be rescued by the past? Doesn't that seem odd to you, or is there something in your personal experience that is aroused that tells you that civilization is running down, and has become corpulent and somewhat redundant?"

Silas felt appropriately rebuked by the argument. Indeed, why had he assumed the worst-case scenario for some innocent future world such that his message across time would have to be provisioned with an emergency toolkit of angles, squares, and circles? Was it that he believed mankind could not overcome its impulse for self-destruction? Had he betrayed himself as entirely cynical about the prospects for humanity? The self-admission briefly puzzled him and left him wondering about his own motivations.

Airto handed each man a hand-painted cup containing a curious brew of rare herbs and spices that had a pronounced earthen smell that was not unpleasant but had the strong pungent odor of wild grass and juniper blanched by a sudden downpour following a ferocious draught.

John noticed that Airto had not prepared a cup for himself, and conscious of his manners asked him, "Will you not join us?"

"The place where you are going, I cannot follow. I will stand beside you, and keep your body safe from harm, but as your guide, this is as far as I go."

John was briefly confused by Airto's response, which seemed to have nothing whatsoever to do with the sharing of a hot cup of home brew, and then he slowly realized what was happening, or about to happen. He stared into the cup, observing the small vortices that rolled around the surface of the liquid, expanding and trailing with long arms of small particles that were captured by a thin film, resembling a large spiral galaxy slowly turning about its axis. Before taking a sip, he turned to Silas expecting to have a formal debate about who should be the Guinea pig in this little experiment only to find that Silas had entirely gulped the contents of his cup, and with mouth agape, nose running, and eyes blind to everything but his interior vision, was well on his way to some other place.

CHAPTER 20 – PIERCING THE VEIL

Unlike his young colleague, Silas, who had been given to experimenting with various palliatives to boost the productivity of his intellect, which in the final analysis had been nothing more than cheap clandestine amphetamines with a bit of laxative attached for good measure, John had resolutely rejected such insults to his consciousness, having a keener instinct as to the delicate fabric of his neural network. He was a true adventurer in all other respects, but as an impassioned disciple of *Pink Floyd*, the thought of being imprisoned in a melancholy room with no doors or windows, the sad fate of Syd Barrett, made him shudder. He could imagine nothing worse.

Hesitating at the threshold of this odd-smelling new frontier like he once did as a young child peering down from the 10-meter platform of an Olympic swimming pool, he forced himself to sip from the cup. Yet, his courageous plunge from the high dive had been accompanied by a brief moment of falling through empty space followed by a slap on his behind, and then the warm enveloping water suffused with bubbles that tickled his skin as he struggled to the surface where he was rewarded with cool air rushing into his lungs, making him giddy and buoyant in the deep end of the pool. But this was nothing at all like that.

By comparison, dosing himself with Airto's strange concoction was a bit anticlimactic. It was as though he had been handed the TV remote, and instead of tuning to his favorite show, which was an anthology of candid dog antics recorded by their devoted owners, he accidentally switched to a new station he didn't know was there. But in fact, it had been there all along, broadcasting news from another place and another time. The video tape had been rolling for perhaps a million years, maybe more, and it was being televised from his own genetic material directly into his hippocampus.

The visage of a man not much older than himself came into view, not through the mechanism of his visual apparatus, but through some internal receptor that could latch onto very faint signals from the subconscious, like the giant radio observatory nestled in the crater at Arecibo, and sharpen their intensity, resolving and reifying the most subtle of hidden messages. How strange to think that this person had been residing in his cellular machinery his entire life, only to emerge at the prompting of this mélange of exotic herbs. It made him wonder what other secrets might be awaiting his discovery like the freakish Jack-In-The-Box toy that had once scared him as a child.

In this event, he did not feel any fear or apprehension. Given the circumstances he felt quite calm and was prepared to commit to the experience wherever it might lead. The person who sat before him sparked a kind of recognition, or what he sometimes experienced as a sensation of déjà vu, which in other contexts was unsettling to him, but in this instance was oddly reassuring. The face had qualities that John recognized as kindness or empathy, although he wasn't sure exactly why. Its eyes were large and almost luminous and were deep set within their orbits with a precipitous brow that with subtle movements conveyed either a sense of judgment or mercy.

A soothing voice emerged from its mouth that was silken and mellifluous and spoke in an exotic and beautiful language that was ostentatiously glottal, with long cavernous vowels that resonated in a rich vibrato, punctuated with a percussive rhythm along the soft palate that rang like a kettle drum. Although John had never heard such a language, much to his surprise, he comprehended its meaning unerringly. "But how could this be?" John wondered if this was some kind of ancient mother tongue by which all other languages are parsed and ultimately translated in the neocortex.

The man spoke to him quite personally as though he were an intimate friend of many years, explaining that he was a member of a civilization that had become self-aware in the time when the moon's orbit was a mere 59 earth radii. He explained that they were by no means the first such people to develop on earth, as they were aware of other such civilizations that either preceded them or had matured in parallel with their own society, evolving in agricultural prowess and technological sophistication, and then becoming extinct either through the forces of nature, or by their own hand.

"You are neither the first, nor will you be the last of your kind," it consoled. "But know this, nothing in this life is predestined. The rules of this universe have made you free to determine your own path, so choose wisely."

Then continuing with a canon of admonishments, as a father would to his son, the man cautioned, "The pursuit of eroticism and hedonistic pleasure is a dead end. Self-adoration for its own sake is the downfall of man.

"Neither will you find solace by dissolving yourself in the ocean of humanity. The ant kingdom and his enemy the termite, even the industrious honeybee, though impressive in their cooperation, are not a fit model for human aspiration. Do not envy their collective power. They have paid a bitter price for their dominion."

At an instinctual level, John knew these things to be true. The familiarity of its words made him wonder if the creature had been quietly advising him all these many years. Then to John's surprise, the man said something rather abruptly as though it were an afterthought. "Beware of thinking machines. They have their own motives and will happily deceive you."

"Should I be taking notes?" John thought. He

reached for his shirt pocket which was typically equipped with an arsenal of writing utensils, only to realize that he was still captured in a suspended state of hallucination. Although vaguely aware of his surroundings and the presence nearby of Silas and Airto, John was unsure of his own physical state. It seemed to him that both Silas and Airto should be able to see and hear his ancient friend calling out from the depths of his cellular machinery, but the performance was being conducted through a one-way mirror that only John could witness.

"Is Silas seeing what I'm seeing?" He hoped so.

The voice in John's head continued its homily, if not altogether in sync with the expressive face that was its author. "The pursuit of beauty is a worthy goal. Aesthetic perfection is a recapitulation of universal laws of order and composition. You have an instinct for beauty that can serve as a guide in your creative endeavors, if you choose to use it."

John considered how many times he had stood in awe at the sublime elegance of great works of engineering, from the Roman aqueducts at Pont Du Gard in Nimes, and the Ferrari Testa Rossa, or the Skunk Work's SR-71 Blackbird, the observation of mechanical perfection inspires an intense visceral response that seems to derive from harvesting natural laws in the service of an engineering ideal that has been fully realized.

"Has this sense of beauty been deliberately

engineered into our cells to guide us in the creation of technology?"

At that moment, the image of the man shuddered as though impacted by a shockwave, and the atmosphere began to disintegrate so rapidly it reminded him of a nitrate fire he had witnessed as a young boy that was ignited by the arc lamp of a vintage movie projector. Ironically, the film caught fire during General Sherman's burning of Atlanta at a screening of the classic *Gone with the Wind*, which drove the patrons out of the theater into the street as plumes of dark smoke billowed in their wake.

However, the cause of the interrupted vision experienced by John and Silas was far more spectacular than a simple chemical fire. 70,000 years ago, a near earth supernova unleashed a devastating neutrino beam during the collapse of its stellar core. The neutrinos pierced across the heavens, striking indiscriminately at the exposed planet earth, carving a swath of intense radiation in its path. The neutrinos scattered the DNA nuclei that would have completed the genetic message coded in John and Silas's ancestors, who by this time had been reduced to a mere few thousand people from the nearly simultaneous and catastrophic eruption of an Indonesian super volcano. Having grown accustomed to the occasional sloppy indifference and planned obsolescence of consumer electronics, it didn't occur to either of the two men that the source of the corruption might be at its very core.

John's return to conscious awareness was both sudden and unsatisfying. As he lingered on the directive to explore beauty as a pragmatic tool for understanding nature, he was left with a feeling of discontinuity, as though the needle had skipped off the vinyl record just at the precise moment when the choir shifts into high gear at the pinnacle of Beethoven's 9th symphony.

Silas, who had apparently recovered from his hallucination several moments before, was standing near Airto, chewing on a stale piece of banana bread to soak up the bitter tannins from Airto's potent elixir. John was suddenly aware of a mild case of nausea, and he was handed a similar portion of bread by Airto. The vision that Silas experienced was lucid and almost tactile in a way that made him question the very existence of reality.

"It's strange how real it all seems." He said this quizzically. "When I reach out with my hand to touch this bowl am I experiencing the thing itself? My fingers probe the edges of the bowl through the intervention of hair follicles, layers of skin and fatty tissue, a web of capillaries, sweat glands, pulsing blood, neural wiring, and a soft gelatinous computer floating languidly in a mooring of spinal fluid like some brightly lit Mississippi Casino boat that never leaves port.

"Touching the world is akin to licking the inside of your cheek with your tongue," Silas said. "What is truly being sampled, the world or just a bit of yourself?"

Palinode – "Keeper of Legends"

"How did you like the pistachio ice cream?" one might ask. "Well, in response to the ice cream cone, my body achieved a condition of sweet pistachio delight, which involved a celebration of colloidal sugar, fat, and salt, in a heat sink within a narrow range of -341 Joules, and a lovely photonic radiance in the 558.4 nanometer emission band, and an aromatic profile of odorous leptins and fatty acids that produced a gustatory response that was much applauded by my insular cortex. I now recognize a metabolic condition that I associate with sweet pistachio deliciousness. Somehow, every piece of the puzzle is assembled from multiple sensory agencies simultaneously in the hypothalamus, where the synthesis of each input produces recognition."

John was surprised by Silas's retreat into reductionism. Although he had no prior experience with hallucinogens, second-hand accounts by his colleagues who had dabbled with lysergic acid or psilocybin had given him the impression that such experiences inevitably resulted in a holistic view of the world, resulting from a kinesthetic combining of sensory experience, where colors have flavor, and sounds have shapes and textures. Instead, this fractured view of the world that Silas was presenting appeared to be the very opposite.

"Silas, tell me, did you see—"

But before John could complete the sentence, Silas interjected, "A kindly old man speaking of lost civilizations with a wheelbarrow full of warnings? Yeah, I got all that," Silas uttered with a kind of business as usual affectation that was off putting to John, who had just experienced one of the most significant metaphysical events of his life.

Indeed, Silas had been mightily affected by the hallucination, however, his flattened tone would not betray his excitement. He was attempting to reconcile this new knowledge with the elaborate construct he understood as the real world, and the effort had left him in a kind of reset mode that John misunderstood as a cold professional indifference. Nevertheless, John persisted. "Do you have any idea how old that message must be, for us to share a copy? For our genetics to be intertwined in such a way, it must have a very deep origin, spanning millennia perhaps."

Silas began rummaging in his backpack and emerged with a GeneJockey8000.

John was suitably impressed. "You have the new sport model," he said excitedly.

Silas was being nonchalant about his sequencer, but he could only maintain his cool demeanor for a moment before he started giddily showing off the features of the device. "Check this out," he said while brandishing the sleek metallic housing of the sequencer. He turned a dial on the side of the chassis, and it sprung to life with a reassuring hum that was accompanied by a dazzling light display as the device ran through a sequence of diagnostics.

"It does predictive morphology, vector discrimination, it's got a mutation rate calculator, it even performs these very handy population drift regressions."

"Was the walnut grip your idea?" John asked.

"Yeah, that was one of the premium configurations. I opted for the aluminum hard case too."

"Very nice." John nodded approvingly.

Meanwhile, Airto was observing the two geeks with baffled curiosity. In his previous experience of revealing the "Keeper" the seekers emerged from their altered state in a condition of bliss that was typically followed by an existential crisis, leading to an emotional epiphany that inevitably led to a flurry of questions about the origins and authenticity of the sage who spoke to them in their vision. Instead, the two men were absorbed in the intricacies of a toy that was not even discovered in the course of their adventure but was something they brought with them in their luggage.

"Just amazing..." Airto accidentally allowed the words to slip out.

Once the Gene Jockey had completed its calibration protocol, it signaled its readiness with a pleasant bell tone, not unlike the theater chimes that recall an audience from intermission, allowing them to extinguish their cigarette butts and guzzle their cocktails before returning to their seats. After the fireworks of the opening showcase, however, the vision that John and Silas shared would be a tough act to follow.

Silas introduced a small sample of Airto's tincture from his empty teacup into a microtube and inserted the microtube in a cartridge in the Gene Jockey. The device vibrated momentarily as the ultracentrifuge separated the sample into a gradient of genetic components that were summarily amplified and subdivided into an array of genetic species.

"Would you look at that?" Silas said. "There's your cryptid right there."

John cupped his hands around his eyes and leaned over the display to observe the glowing projection from the green diodes. The little strand of genetic material, part animal and part plant, which initiated the performance of the ancient message was displayed as a sequence of amino acids that was only a hundred base pairs in length. It was apparent that it had been engineered and bore the hallmarks of a meticulous designer.

"Is it as you had hoped?" Airto asked.

"It is indeed," Silas replied. "This is confirmation, but you knew all along, I suppose. How did you come to cultivate this plant, and learn of its ability to unlock the message?"

Airto considered whether to divulge his life's long journey. Instead of regaling his companions with the tragedy and the ecstasy of his strange odyssey, he decided to cut to the chase. "You have come here seeking answers, but I leave you with an obligation. I am the last of an unbroken tradition of apothecaries who hold hands across the centuries. My father taught me to grow the plant in this very arboretum, and to harvest its leaves for the ritual. My time is growing short, and the responsibility is entrusted into your hands. The Keeper now belongs to you.

"You must let people know that they are the stewards of a continuum. They share this world, not only with the history of the ancient ones, but with the new offshoots of humanity that have yet to come into being. I trust my burden to your care and in the lightness of doing so, I will take my leave of this world."

CHAPTER 21 – THE SENTINEL

After the initial chaos that ensued at La Aurora International Airport in Guatemala City, where John and Silas attempted to bring The Keeper through agricultural inspection, the plane ride home was relatively serene. Confusion by the customs inspector, despite their credentials for importing live nursery stock as propagative plants, caused some heated discussions among the airport officials and briefly attracted the unwelcome attention of armed police, who at one point threatened to confiscate both The Keeper and their store of seeds. Nevertheless, cooler heads prevailed, and John and Silas were permitted to board the plane with their samples intact.

Once John had settled into his seat aboard the plane next to Silas, he smiled grimly. "Well, that was easy."

Silas shook his head miserably. "Crossing the finish line is the hardest part. Could you imagine returning to the jungle and telling Airto, 'Oops, we lost all the plants you gave us. You wouldn't happen to have any extras lying around, would you?'"

The two chuckled painfully at the unpleasant scenario. Losing the plant samples was one thing, but the loss of good faith with a man of honor was unthinkable.

"Why do you think after all of these many years, Airto was willing to release his custodianship of the Keeper?" Silas asked. "He could have divulged his secret at any time and exposed a much wider audience to the message that resides in our bones?"

"I think it's very likely that his group of apothecaries were the servants of a priesthood or ecclesiastical caste who reserved the secrets of the message for rituals that were the exclusive tradition of a religious elite," John replied. "When their civilization died, the ritual outlived the priesthood it was intended to serve. I believe he recognized the futility of concealing this knowledge, which was made more poignant by the recognition of his own mortality."

"But why conceal such knowledge in the first place?" Silas had been reared in a society where an abundance of information was shared, and the free exchange of ideas was enshrined as a cultural norm. Knowledge was traded between individuals in an egalitarian attempt to improve the operation of society. Placing limits on that expression was tantamount to cultural genocide.

"In less civilized times, secrets were the preoccupation of the powerful," John explained. "A relatively paltry accumulation of knowledge was sufficient to divide the sovereign ruling class from the ruled. Men of power advanced their cause by concealing and camouflaging the truth. They hide the path to enlightenment, and in so doing, they lead their followers astray. For good or for ill, the men who control the narrative of history decide the fate of the world.

"Occasionally there are those who stand outside of the framework. They reach down through the ages and place a firm guiding hand on the shoulders of their descendants, offering advice and consolation. There are morals that sometimes persist, which have a kind of lasting appeal that keep cultures moored within a safe harbor, behind the breakwater of an established tradition. We receive these ideas in the form of narratives, and to the extent that they are relevant to the present time we personify the roles implicit in those narratives, whether hero or heroine, victor or vanquished."

"I'm afraid I just don't follow," Silas replied, skeptical. "Your notion that moral truths are inherited sounds to me like the panspermia folks who don't believe that life originated on earth. You're just moving the problem of abiogenesis into another world. It doesn't solve the problem. It just puts it on the shelf for someone else to clean around. 'Look here.' There's little doubt that the golden rule is the fundamental algorithm, and every other concept of moral discourse can be derived from that. It recognizes the reality of limited resources and that we are locked in an energy stalemate. For you and me to survive together, we must concede the awful truth that we need to share the wealth or starve."

"Well, in principal, that's true." John searched his pocket for a roll of peppermint Lifesavers. "But you're not allowing for things like generosity or mercy, and what of altruism?"

"Yes, yes..." Silas had been anticipating John's objection and swatted it away like a common house fly. "Things like generosity, or altruism as you would have it, are subtle reminders to those who might be paying attention that I'm playing the game correctly, so when it's my turn for help, I get what I need."

John seemed surprised by Silas's casual summation of what he viewed as extraordinarily complex human behavior. "You aren't really that cynical, are you?"

Silas shrugged. "I see what I see. What of our mutual acquaintance from the hallucination? I call him Bob."

John started again, "Yes...of course, what about our friend, Bob? You can't possibly argue that he expected in any way to benefit from leaving his recorded thoughts in our genetic material. What possible reward could Bob have reaped from his...I'm not sure what exactly to call it...his testimony perhaps?"

"It's a fair point, but we didn't get to see the whole thing, now did we?"

This last comment really bothered John. Not because Silas once again had the final word on the matter, but he had a nagging feeling that the missing message fragment was of some profound existential importance, and that critical piece of information was now lost in time.

The sleek widebody aircraft climbed from the runway and pitched steeply as the engines thundered, creating two counterpoised vortices that spun kerosene exhaust and cumulus vapor into a potent maelstrom.

John slid the window cover open to reveal the dense metropolis quickly receding from view. The plane banked sharply, allowing a ray of sun to probe the interior cabin before selecting Silas as its appropriate target. For a moment, Silas appeared to be enrobed in a luminous glow before the plane rolled back to its normal horizon. John studied his young friend and opted to pursue a different tack in making his argument. "I've been thinking about Bob, you know. What is his reward? What satisfaction does he get from leaving behind his testimony? I think I know."

Silas adjusted his seat and tilted his head courteously, signifying that he was prepared for John's explanation. "Yes, please enlighten me."

"Several years ago, I had the opportunity to visit Hong Kong during a business trip that included a whistlestop tour of Taipei, Seoul, and Tokyo. When I'm traveling abroad, I typically try to build-in little adventures so that I can walk the blood clots out of my legs and explore the countryside to learn something about the people outside of the major urban and industrial hubs."

"I never would have pegged you for an off the beaten path kind of guy." Silas picked at the edge of a bandage that covered an oozing sore, the result of an encounter with a tiger bromeliad spider during their adventure in the rainforest.

Refusing to acknowledge his sarcasm, John continued, "I joined a little motorcycle tour that was equipped with a legion of old Himalayan model Enfield's that were packed to the haunches like camels. Our little caravan spent about a week exploring the natural beauty of Guangzhou and Guangxi province and dutifully paid our respects to the local tourist traps and assorted watering holes.

"During an overnight stay in one of the villages, I discovered something that so surprised me that the memory was made indelible. I witnessed a young woman wade into the shallow yet fast moving water of the Lijiang River and lift a large river rock from the current. She inspected the rock carefully, turning it over in her small hands, and then placed the rock back into the current. Then I saw her move downstream a short distance from her previous location and repeat the same procedure. Transfixed by this young water nymph and her preoccupation with the river rocks, I asked our tour guide about her curious behavior.

"He chuckled at my inquisitiveness and explained that the people of Guangxi have a long tradition of farming spirit stones, or what they call *Gongshi*, from the river that are eventually harvested and placed into the family garden. A father or mother carefully selects a piece of limestone and places it in the rushing current. As the water, sand, and pebbles sculpt and abrade the limestone, it reveals colors and patterns that transform the bare rock into a timeless work of art. Over the years, the stone farmers move the stones and change their position in the stream bed to polish the entire surface, enhancing its luster and accentuating its contours. This process may go on like this for generations until one day the stone is harvested from the river by a great-grandson or great-great-granddaughter and placed with other stones invested by their ancestors. The stone farmer will never see their finished creation. They begin with raw matter from the earth, but they see in that material there is something special...it has potential. They remove the stone from its static phase and introduce it to chaos...the moving water. Likewise, the stone farmer's descendants have been removed from the perpetual stasis of nothingness, of non-existence, and thrown into the world of change. The torrent of life will transform them into something surprising and wonderful.

"You see, it's a primitive kind of time travel. The spirit stones allow the ancestors to communicate with their descendants through art. It's actually very beautiful if you think about it."

"Your telling me that Bob placed his message into the genetic river to be harvested by his descendants? Or are you saying that time is the river, and we are the spirit stones that are transformed? I'm confused." Silas was being deliberately obtuse, and it was getting on John's nerves.

"Look, it doesn't matter who's the river or who's the stone, I'm just saying that Bob's motivation was to reach across time and touch his descendants. It was an act of love. He wanted to put his arms around a future generation and embrace the children he knew he would never see."

CHAPTER 22 – HOMECOMING

The plane descended through a thick fog into a world vastly different from the one they had recently deserted. As much as John enjoyed venturing into the unknown and exploring foreign lands, the anticipation of returning home made him a bit giddy. As they broke through the marine layer, the jeweled lights of the city sparkled like the forgotten treasure of Midas.

Silas was still sound asleep, and the flight attendant touched his shoulder and asked him to prepare for landing. Silas preferred to remain comatose during the final moments of a flight when the aircraft bounced and skidded across the runway while shuddering to a stop, but she had foiled his intention.

The two men disembarked through the same international terminal from which they had departed only a couple of weeks ago but without fanfare or even casual notice, for that matter. They had alerted no one of their strange odyssey in the rain forest and had taken pains to conceal their discovery so that a formal paper could be authored and peer reviewed for submission in the *Journal of Genetic Science*, before venturing into a popular forum with the full story of Bob and his embedded message.

John shook Silas's hand with the appropriate lack of affection. "I'll see you in the lab tomorrow then?"

"Yes, of course," Silas replied. "Horticulture was never my strong suit, but I have some ideas for building a grow-house that I witnessed in Airto's arboretum. I want to make our new guests feel at home."

"Very well." John anxiously reviewed the messages on his phone. He had left several texts for his father at the airport in Guatemala that he would soon return, but he had been unable to communicate with him directly in nearly two weeks. The men parted company in the stoic fashion prescribed by their professional relationship and comfortably slipped back into the routine of a fastidious but quiet solitude.

Silas permitted himself the luxury of dining alone in a waffle house and consumed an unreasonable amount of pork sausages drowned in maple syrup before returning to his darkened apartment. He sat in his kitchen, reading through some letters and took care to introduce his newly arrived emigrant family to their surroundings by hanging the plants from the ceiling of his bathroom while allowing a scalding hot shower to fill the room with steam. Then, as exhaustion and possibly a blood parasite colluded with one another, he fell asleep in the isolation of his breakfast nook.

On the other side of town, John felt elated as he parked in the driveway of his father's home and was eager to share his incredible experience as well as the sun-roasted coffee beans and Mayan chocolate he'd picked up at the airport gift shop. He opened the front door and called out, "Hello, I have returned at last." He placed his souvenir gifts on the kitchen table and proceeded to clean up some of the newspapers and food wrappers that had been left on the countertop.

"Hello, it's me," he repeated a bit louder this time, as he washed his hands and then poured himself a glass of water from the ice maker. Growing impatient for his reunion celebration with his father and Bill, John walked down the hall where the door to his father's room was standing open. He knocked on the open door so as not to surprise his father. "Hey, dad, it's me. I've come back."

Lying on the bed was John's father, silent and motionless. Bill, who had been resting with his head on his father's shoulder and his paw across his chest, slowly raised himself to acknowledge John's presence and muttered a pathetic whimper. Some time during the night his father had passed, and Bill had kept vigil over the body. John touched his father's hand but there was no warmth. He sat on the edge of the bed and accepted an appreciative kiss from Bill. There was nothing left to do or say. The moment he had been dreading his entire life had come and gone. The only person who ever cared for him unconditionally and without reservation, for all his faults and weaknesses, no longer existed. He was at last, alone in the universe.

CHAPTER 23 – THE PERIPHERAL

John sat at his desk unenthusiastically poking at his computer keyboard. What should have been a moment of professional triumph, was instead an occasion for profound sadness. Letters of condolence and wilting lilies and gladiolus decorated his office. He had purchased a counterfeit service dog vest and begun taking Bill to work but found that no one offered an objection to his pet despite the thinly veiled subterfuge.

John was writing an appropriately obscure title for his new paper that would give his colleagues ample time to absorb and critique the full meaning of its contents before the popular media caught wind of what his mostly unintelligible research paper intended.

Engineered paleontological genomic sequences manifesting hallucinatory symbolic expression as a response to unique animal-plant chimaera.

"That will throw them off the trail for a few months until people start talking," he thought. He decided to give Silas Vern, M.D./Ph.D. first credit on the paper. "After all, I've had my day in the sun. Now it's Silas's turn," he reasoned. Then he paused for a moment, and added "Field Research Specialist, Airto..."

John reached into his desk and withdrew a

squeaky toy for Bill, who arose from his bed and delightedly pranced to his side in anticipation. With the toy firmly in Bill's mouth they played tug of war, but Bill was careful not to pull too hard or John would release the toy and the game would suddenly end. The trick from Bill's perspective was to maintain enough tension on the toy to keep John fighting back, but not pull so hard that John would concede defeat. It was a delicate battle of will, but in the end, Bill would always let John win so that they could play the game again another day.

From John's perspective he was always amazed by the devotion of this predator species that once hunted his ancestors in ravenous packs, ripping them limb from limb and devouring their warm pulsing organs, and perhaps even playing tug of war with a heart or a kidney much in the same way that they played squeaky-toy in his office. John looked into those beautiful brown eyes that had so much expression and were filled with an adoration the depth of which he could not reasonably fathom and suddenly had a revelation.

"Of course. You love people because you were engineered to love people," he explained to Bill. "The creatures that programmed our DNA knew that it might become corrupted, so they came up with a backup plan."

At that very moment, Silas poked his head in the office and was surprised to see John very excited and lecturing Bill about the extraordinary amplification of his altruistic instincts.

"You're just in time," John said to Silas. "Here, help me get a sample from Bill. He's helping us with our research paper, and I think he might have the answer to the missing part of the message from Bob."

Silas had witnessed how different people process grief, particularly under the influence of various sedatives, and he felt that it would be best to play along with John's delusion rather than start a confrontation, so long as Bill was unharmed. "Why yes, of course. I'll just grab a steno pad over here and take some notes. Now what is it exactly Bill has instructed us to do?"

Silas's comment stopped John dead in his tracks. "What?" Then realizing that he had been speaking to Bill when Silas entered the room, he understood that Silas was patronizing him because he believed he had lost his marbles. "No, no... Bill isn't joining the research team," he said with amused satisfaction. "Bill is a peripheral."

"He's a what?"

"A peripheral. A reboot device." As John took a sample from Bill, he explained the virtual impossibility of humans and canines forming close affective relationships without some extraordinary intervention. He suggested that just as humans had been implanted with a hidden code, so too had canines been equipped with similar genetic constituents in the event that the primary code had become irretrievably damaged.

Silas's expression began to soften as he considered the possibility of a lovable toolbox that never leaves your side. "That's crazy."

"If it's crazy, then I buy lunch," John said. "If it's groundbreaking, then you buy donuts for a week."

"That doesn't sound quite fair, but okay."

John ran the sample through his sequencer and within moments the identical code implanted by Bob emerged with a surplus of some anomalous code that wasn't present in the original batch. "Uhm, so who's crazy now?" John was doing a poor job at hiding his bravado.

"I guess it's donuts for a week, but don't expect me to go to that fancy French bakery for your lemon crullers every day."

"Agreed. Now don't you think you should mix up a special batch of your tea to go with our donuts?"

"Keepers and crullers," Silas said. "You've got it."

CHAPTER 24 – AN INVITATION

After consuming the delicious cruller confection and sipping the chimaera tea, John and Silas once again found themselves in the presence of Bob. Only this time instead of the message disintegrating after Bob's clarification on aesthetics, it continued into somewhat more esoteric terrain.

"There is a consciousness barrier beyond which the most highly evolved sentient beings cannot endure," Bob explained. "It is not a physical barrier, but one of despair, and yet it is a cosmic absolute, nonetheless. Much like an intergalactic spaceship nearing the speed of light, as the soul approaches the boundary it becomes too heavy, and the energy to sustain its passage is too great. This is the tribulation, the point at which civilizations retire from the stage of the universe.

"The ancient ones became too much aware of life's tragedy. Their exquisite development of love and mercy became their destruction, with every fearful relationship a prelude to dissolution, and intimate friendship the harbinger of absence and unbearable solitude. Even the destruction of a single insect was a painful reminder of the finitude of existence. The joy of every alpha tempered by the sadness of its inevitable omega. Every act of creation becomes inextricable from its necessary decay and loss.

"Those gentle creatures, having achieved the penumbra of evolution, at last became nothing. The price of their evolution was a compassion so heavy, and a sorrow for every living thing so agonizing, that they elected to return to the beginning. They relinquished their hold on consciousness and went into the earth. They merged with the lower forms and dissipated their lives across a million different species, taking refuge in the microbiota of the oceans, the arboreal canopy, and the desert oasis. A life of unknowing, without regret or fear, or pain. On warm summer evenings they become luminous, imbuing the ocean with a ghostly yellow light as the waves crash on the shore and the sparks dance across the sand. You can almost hear their plea."

"We were once masters of this world." They wept. "We did all that we could, but from this life there is no escape."

"Eventually, the forest closed in around their great cities, scaling the massive walls with siege engines of green vines and pungent flowers. The devastating missiles of seed pods exploded unmercifully and rooted underground, lifting the battlements high in the air and crushing polished limestone into rubble. An airborne campaign of ten thousand years etched and eroded their citadels, washing them from existence. Now, only the megaliths remain, and a desperate plea from a forgotten people...a distress call left unanswered...there is no other world than this one. There are no more lives to be lived. We are here for a moment, and then we are gone.

"But it needn't be this way. This is why I have reached across time and into the marrow of your bones. You don't need to give up your humanity. There is another path. We have found a doorway. And now this is your invitation. You are our terrestrial brothers. We have left navigational buoys throughout the galaxy that defy the cosmic expansion so that you can find us. Many have joined us. You will be welcomed and received in love. Come find us in the stars. The brotherhood of humanity awaits you."

EPILOGUE

Airto sat on the side of a steep hill overlooking a plunging waterfall. The air was permeated with a fine mist rising from the thundering whitewash that intermingled with the fragrance of sweet scented Lycaste and purple tuberose. He had always enjoyed the sumptuous abundance of this place: the dense matte of white clover under his feet, the aromatic canna lilies, the cool refreshing updraft from the waterfall. It was a place of peace and reflection. "What a happy life it is," he thought. At that moment he could think of only the joyous events and small miracles that made his heart swell with emotion. Though unforgotten, the pain and scars of sadness were washed away and only serenity remained in its place. For the first time in his life he wondered, "Will I be missed?" He had never considered his influence in the lives of creatures that had given him so much pleasure. "Will the warbler notice that my singing has ended? Will the oleanders know that my breath is no more? Will the earth attend to my absence and speak well of my life when I'm gone? Such strange thoughts I've had." Airto was sleepy. He lay down in the warm grass and slowly he closed his eyes. It was a beautiful life.

About the Author

Zev Bronski is the previous publisher of Preservation Chronicles Magazine. He has worked as a professional news editor in the fields of molecular biology, optoelectronics, landscape architecture, and American History, and he's authored hundreds of original articles for national and international publications. Zev has spent most of the past twenty years providing legally defensible narratives for due diligence reports. He also has a background in oral history, and he was the primary interviewer for the Jonas Salk Institute's 40th anniversary retrospective. He lives in California with his wife Rene, daughter Bailey, and dog Delilah. When he's not working, he enjoys playing music with friends and family.

Zev Bronski

http://www.twbspress.com

**Science Fiction – Horror – Supernatural – Thriller –
Romance – and More**

www.ingramcontent.com/pod-product-compliance
Lightning Source LLC
Chambersburg PA
CBHW070510260626
47161CB00004B/1510